KRISTOPHER JEROME

THE GODS AND MEN CYCLE

TEARS OF THE GODLESS

THE BROKEN PACT
BOOK 3

Cover art by Sanjin Halimic

Cover design by Miblart

Maps by Ralarismaps

Illustration by Patrick Buermeyer

Hardcover ISBN: 978-1-951138-18-9

Paperback ISBN: 978-1-951138-20-2

ALSO FROM DARK TIDINGS PRESS

THE GODS AND MEN CYCLE

By Kristopher Jerome

The Broken Pact Trilogy:

- Wrath of the Fallen
- Cries of the Forsaken
- Tears of the Godless

The Nightbreaker

White Wings from Grey Ash

Before the Breaking:

- A Bandit's Balance
- A Voice from the Darkness
- In the Shadow of Light
- The Sons of Lighthammer
- The Bard's Demons
- Disciples of the First Cycle
- Ten of Seatown
- The Last Gift of Kane Darksend
- The Grey God's Edict
- The Blood-Soaked Sacrament

For my wife Stephanie. My biggest fan and greatest champion. I love you Mo Anam Cara.

Artorus
The Rim of Paradise
Lioss
The Grey Temple
Rinwarthe
Eligan
Pyeth
Seatown
Kliwen
Amel
Streta
Illux
The Great Chasm
Ostarth
Ryun
The Nameless Sea
Firan
Marna
The High God's Tears
Godsend

The Grey God's Shrine
Ayyslid
The High God's Throne
The Basin
Infernaak

"We must stamp out all the Darkness we find, even that in
our own hearts. In this, above all else, we must not falter."

— LIO, GOD OF LIGHT ADDRESSING HIS TROOPS AT
CREATOR'S REST, 124 AC

TEARS OF THE GODLESS

PROLOGUE

1054 AP

The gates of Illux swung open ominously. Ahead, Tess nodded to the Captain of the City Watch, drawing her sword. She charged forward, with the battalions of Demigods following closely behind her. Fenris was one such Demigod, nestled back toward the rear of the column. He thought fear would grip him as they exited the safety of the city, but to his surprise, he was relatively calm. After all, he had faced death out near the Great Chasm and felt true fear out there. He had survived that horror, and that was before he had consumed *the blood*.

It was still surreal to him, the power that now flowed in his veins. Tess had returned from the battlefield, telling the other survivors, soldier and Paladin alike, that she had found and consumed some of the Goddess Arra's silver blood. It had healed her wounds, and given her strength and the power to create ice. At first, they balked at her claim—until she proved her power. Fenris had been one of the first to follow her back to the wellspring and imbibe the power.

A white streak of his previously dark hair hung in front of his eyes. He pushed it aside with the back of his hand. He had yet to visit his family and let them know that he had survived the battle, let alone what he had become afterward. Demigods hadn't been welcomed back with open arms by the people of Illux or the Paladins that ran the city. Fenris feared what would happen if his mother and father saw the lone white streak in his hair, or what they would think when they saw what he could do now.

If we survive this assault, I will find them. Before the walls are breached.

Beyond the walls of Illux, the surrounding plains had become a gauntlet of death and destruction. Demons and Accursed did battle with one another in the distance, just out of the reach of the gates. Divine Beasts from the sky swooped lower here and there, breathing flame or ice down onto the embattled forces. It was chaos made manifest. It was exactly what Tess had been hoping for.

"This way!" she shouted. Tess motioned for them to make their way toward the flank of one of the two armies. "We hit them hard and then we get our asses back inside!"

Fenris swallowed. He had been a fresh recruit to the army just before the Seraph Ren had led them out of the city those few weeks ago. Some of his companions were veterans, used to taking orders from Tess for the last few years. Fenris simply followed her because he could think of nothing else to do. She had given him this *gift*, after all.

As they drew near the closest cluster of Demons and Accursed, Fenris pulled his mace free and cleared his mind. Tess had reminded each of them that once they used their powers they would be giving up the element of surprise, so each attack needed to count. Fenris didn't expect his gifts to be particularly useful against the enemies on the ground, but against those in the air…

"Now!" Tess shouted.

Her body, already covered in shards of ice, shot out a frozen burst that covered the entire rear guard of the enemy, freezing most of the Accursed and some of the Demons solid. The Demigods swarmed over them, shattering their foes with several well-placed strikes. A frozen Demon loomed over Fenris as he entered the fray. He slammed his mace into its helm, shattering the great beast in one blow.

I wish they could all be that easy.

Lightning arced over his head, hammering into the first Demon to realize the danger the Demigods posed. Fenris ducked a little lower and pushed ahead, stumbling over a fallen corpse. He tripped and rolled to a stop at the feet of an Accursed. This one wasn't frozen. The fallen Demigod screamed as he smashed the knees of the creature with his mace, jumping back to his feet while it fell. One more strike from his mace dented its skull with a wet crunch. He looked up to see dozens of the creatures converging on him.

"Gods have mercy," he sighed.

Rocks burst from the ground in front of him, forming a protective barrier of stone. Several Accursed found themselves impaled on the sharp edges of the stony wall. A woman called Dorea sprang beside him, arms outstretched. As if by command, more stones rose where she pointed, knocking a wave of the enemy back. She flashed Fenris a wicked smile.

"Don't get yourself killed too quickly, now," she said. "We never had that ale."

Then she was gone, leaving Fenris blushing behind the rocky barrier. He would need to buy her several rounds to make up for that one. He scanned the battlefield. The Demigods were spread thin already; their surprise advance had punched quite a dent into the enemy forces, but that meant that they were getting farther and farther from the gate. By now the Demons had realized what was happening and were trying to muster a response. Thankfully, the Divine Beasts were still ignoring them, and the Herald seemed to be engaged elsewhere.

Could there be another Herald leading this rival force? Is that possible?

A Demon bounded over the upraised stones, black flame launching from its free hand. Fenris ran to the left, just as the ground where he had been standing erupted. Another Demigod jumped up to meet the creature, a man named Orrin. Orrin's hands were glowing white hot as he punched into the Demon, shattering through its breastplate. Even so, its black sword swung through the air, severing both of the man's arms at the elbow. He cried out and collapsed, blood spurting everywhere.

The fear from the battle near the Great Chasm returned to Fenris in a wave. He was reminded that even with all of their power, these Demigods were still simply mortals. Mortals who had no chance against the overwhelming odds outside these walls. He turned to run back toward the others, hoping to lose the image of the dying Orrin that was burned into his mind. He saw that Tess had begun to gather others to her again. It looked as if they were preparing to return to the wall. Now that the Demons had realized what they were up against, the resistance had grown too strong.

As he ran back toward his commander, Fenris still scanned the sky for signs of a Divine Beast attacking from above. All of the ground-dwelling creatures were safely in the distance, fighting for their respective armies well away from where the Demigods now clustered. Suddenly, a great shadow passed over him. The Demigod warrior looked up to see what looked like a giant, twisted bird, winging its way toward Tess and the others. His stomach felt as if it had fallen from his body.

Fenris stopped running, dropping his mace and shield into the dirt. He raised his arms over his head and clawed at the sky, trying to bend it to his will. Black clouds formed above them, funneling downward toward his fingertips. Lightning split the sky from within the dark spiral, drawing looks from all over the battlefield.

Fenris twisted his fingers and the clouds responded, snaking their way toward the Divine Beast.

The wind began to howl, a deafening gale that helped to usher the dark clouds along to their final destination. A burst of lightning, larger than any other, shot out of the clouds and struck the Divine Beast with a thunderous crack. The creature cried out, twisting back in the direction of Fenris. Then the funneling clouds enveloped the bird, striking it with lightning again and again. The winds crescendoed and the creature was thrown from the sky. It landed in the distance, taking out dozens of Demons and Accursed as it smashed into the earth.

Fenris fell to his knees as the winds died down and the clouds dissipated. He had never used his powers to that extreme before. The most he had done on their journey back to Illux was manipulate the weather to keep their trip dry.

That was amazing. I did that.

He immediately vomited up his breakfast. The effort had taken everything from him. It was at that moment that he realized that he could not make himself stand. Hands pulled him to his feet. He looked over to see that Dorea was the one dragging him to salvation. A deep gash ran along her hairline, causing crimson blood and dirt to stain her face. Her previous smirk was replaced with a grimace.

"*Two* fucking ales," she said.

They left his mace and shield in the muck behind them as they limped to safety. His strength started to return enough that he no longer needed to put all of his weight on her. They returned to the cluster forming around Tess, the fearless commander keeping the enemy at bay with the force of a blizzard.

"We wait until everyone is back," Tess shouted. "Then we return to the gate. Those of you who can, hold them off." Her eyes fell on Dorea and Fenris. "Don't think you're exempt, Fenris. We all saw what you did."

A cheer rose up from the ranks. Fenris felt his cheeks get hot. Someone shouted and pointed to the sky. Overhead it looked as if three winged shapes engaged in a fierce battle. Leathery wings held these human-sized creatures aloft. It seemed that his previous fear had been correct. Now there were *three* Heralds. Three. Behind the Heralds, several more Divine Beasts started to fly in this direction.

"Gods," Dorea whispered. "We should get going, I think."

Fenris saw the look of pain that crossed Tess' face. She wasn't one to leave anyone behind. Rumor was that one of her Paladin sisters had died in the battle of the Great Chasm. Now she thought of each of her warriors as family, and she didn't want to go through that again. Tess finally nodded.

"Alright, we need to fall back. Edmund will cover our retreat with the ballistae," she paused, "but first, Fenris...take those bastards down." Tess motioned at the Heralds.

Fenris nearly wretched again. He stumbled forward, arms raised. The clouds came to him quicker this time, though he felt his energy sapping even faster than it had before. He snarled and flicked his wrists, sending the black funnel toward the enemy commanders. A wicked bolt of lightning shot out, striking one head-on. It fell to the ground in a smoking heap. The other two turned just as the funnel engulfed them. A scream from behind him broke his concentration. It was Dorea. Fenris collapsed. He turned just in time to see a herd of four-legged creatures bounding toward them. They were the things that the goddess Arra had created from the traitors at the Great Chasm.

Sintaurs, they had named them.

No. Not now.

They looked like twisted goats and dogs, each with haggard human faces pulled too tightly across their skulls. Large fangs protruded from their frothing mouths. The sintaurs sprang into the center of the Demigods, ripping out throats and clawing out eyes. The warriors screamed and broke ranks, running back for the safety of Illux in a mad dash. Tess grabbed Fenris and slung him over her shoulder. Two of the beasts lunged at her, but they were stopped in midair—held aloft by an invisible force. Mikel Drakestone, a longtime companion of Tess' nodded at her, motioning away from them to send the sintaurs flying into another group.

Tess led the fractured group back through the battlefield, dodging sintaurs and Accursed where they could. Finally, they returned to the gate from which they had exited the city, panting and heaving like tired dogs. Tess sat her load down and walked toward the gate. Fenris sighed in relief when he saw that Dorea had made it back with them. She went to work creating a barrier of stone to keep the sintaurs at bay while the Demigods retreated back into the city. Fenris looked around from where Tess had left him. It seemed that they had lost dozens of their companions. Hopefully, some of those were simply separated and would return to the gates to be let inside.

"Open the gate!" Tess shouted.

"Why was it closed in the first place?" Mikel asked.

"Open the gate!"

"Help us!"

But the gate never opened. Fenris sat up just as the Divine Beast landed on the stone perch that Dorea had created for it. It opened its great maw and the world was bathed in fire.

1

It had been hardly a month since Ren had led another army, one much larger than this one, to its eventual demise. The parallel sickened her. Those had been actual warriors—soldiers and Paladins alike. These were just villagers; fishermen, farmers, and the like. She knew that the people of Seatown were hardier than those of Illux, years of attacks from Demons and bandits had seen to that. Even so, she had little hope that they would last long against the enemy, armed as they were.

Their leader, Admiral Wyn Thacker, had sent the young and infirm down the coast to an inlet where they would find shelter and supplies. The looks she had given them as they had left told Ren that she didn't hold much hope for their small army's survival either. Once the group of grandparents and children were receding into the distance, they began their march in earnest. It would take them more than a week to get to Illux with a force of this size, which was time that Ren feared they did not have. She hoped that it would not be too late by the time they arrived at the city.

Traveling with the small army were the massive Divine Beasts, each towering over the Seatown villagers like living mountains. Some kept their distance from the holy creatures, while others felt safer traveling in their shadow. None of them had spoken much to Ren since the battle in the preceding days. They had lost another of their number to the creature called Rullug the Murk; they had lost Orros just as she had lost Trent.

I would have loved you forever.

She didn't allow herself to cry for him. She could not. Grief would destroy her, it would destroy Illux. Ren tightened her grip on the reigns of her horse and galloped ahead. At the front of the column, Gil rode upon Trent's horse, lost in thought. He had only just discovered that his lover Devin had been killed in battle with Akklor the Unbidden, first of the Divine Beasts to be re-awakened. The Seraph slowed her horse next to the Paladin and looked him over. While once a handsome man, Gil now looked worn and hollow. His eyes seemed emptier than she had ever noticed before. It didn't look as if he had even washed the soot or blood off of himself from the last few days. She had to remind herself that he had lost the love of his life, his best friend, and his entire village in these few short weeks as well.

"Gil," she said, softly. "How are you holding up?"

Gil grunted in response. He looked her direction and his gaze softened.

"My lady," he sighed. "My apologies, I was lost in thought."

"I know the feeling."

"I don't know what to do now that both of them are gone," he said. She could see that he was holding back tears. "When Marna burned, I felt lost like I had never felt before. Then I found a purpose. I found Seatown. I did everything I did to try and save Illux, to save our people—but each step of the way, every terrible thing I did, I did to get back to Devin and Trent. Now, I am left with nothing but my guilt."

Ren had gleaned a little of what had transpired before she had arrived in Seatown. It seemed that Gil had led a band of men and women loyal to her against the Ten, the group of Paladins who ruled Seatown with an iron fist. During the small uprising, many had been killed, and by the sounds of it, Gil had shown little mercy to those whom he fought against.

I never should have allowed their heresy to grow.

She had ignored the signs that Seatown was growing restless. They had suffered multiple raids under the previous Seraph Jerrok, from Demons, bandits, and even a rogue Paladin. To appease their growing unrest, Ren had allowed them far more autonomy than any of the other settlements outside of Illux. Her predecessor wouldn't have allowed them to question his rule. She had to remind herself that his ruthlessness had led her to attempt to kill him herself, shortly before the Demons attacked.

"You did what you had to," she said, finally. "All of us have made mistakes in this war, Gil. You stayed loyal to me, and more importantly, you stood up for those being crushed by the grip of the Ten's tyranny. There is no shame in that."

"Tell that to the army that follows you," he said, flatly. "They would speak differently. It was their brothers and sisters burning in those ships."

"Aye, but if those ships had not burned, they would have sailed into the sea, and been slaughtered by those Divine Beasts. None of them would have survived that, and we would be marching to Illux alone."

"And Trent would still live."

His words cut her. She tightened her grip on the reigns again. He was right and she knew it. He had killed the love of her life and left them both alone in the world.

No.

"Trent would have given his life for all of them, whether he made that choice or not is irrelevant. You didn't kill him, the Gods of Darkness did. And soon, we will make them pay for every drop of blood they have spilled. For Trent, and for Devin."

And Arran.

She thought back to her own best friend who had fallen to the same Demons that had slain Jerrok. In twenty years, the wound had still not healed. Arran had been with her every step of her journey, until suddenly she wasn't. If she had Arran with her still, she would have been able to avoid many of the pitfalls that had plagued her rule as Seraph of Illux.

More hoof beats broke her concentration as another horse rode up beside them. Ren turned and saw the swirling blues and greens of the Admiral of Seatown's cloak. Wyn's dark gaze fell upon Gil, a scowl that softened somewhat when the man averted his eyes from her.

"Ren," she said.

"Admiral," Ren replied.

"I wanted to discuss what plans you had for the next few days."

"Such as?"

"Food. We left without many supplies. Foraging will only get us so much. How do you intend to feed my people? A forced march such as this one will decimate us without food. Had you planned for that? Or are you simply trying to expend every last one of us while you try and avenge your lost love?"

Ren tried to keep her anger in check. "We will stop in Amel and take what food they left there. It was the village of my youth. I know that they will have stores of grains and some livestock that they no doubt left behind when I called them behind the walls. Foraging until then will have to be good enough. Wouldn't you agree?"

"Fine. And once we arrive at Illux? What then? If the city hasn't fallen by then, will you throw us against the tide of Demons and Accursed until we are smashed to bits? As I told you when I swore fealty to your cause, I did not pledge my people for a suicide mission."

"Nor have you. When we get closer, our scouts will take stock of the situation. I intend for the Divine Beasts and I to cut a large enough swath that your troops can make it into the city and bolster the forces there. The walls of Illux have never fallen to the Forces of Darkness. They won't now, either."

Wyn nodded and turned her horse about, riding back further into the marching group of villagers. Ren watched her go, noticing the way that those on foot looked at the woman as she rode past. They were just as loyal to the Admiral as the people of Illux were loyal to Ren. Without her, Ren would have no hope of compelling these people to complete the journey to Illux. She would need to truly get the Admiral on her side, somehow.

"She's just posturing," Gil said. "She's a good woman. Wyn did what she could to undercut the atrocities of the Ten. She truly wants what's best for her people. All they want is a land of their own, free of our laws and our problems."

"So she says," Ren replied. "You almost sound like you respect her."

"I do," Gil said. "I tried to get her to join me. Perhaps, if I had tried harder, I could have turned the city without bloodshed. I will never know. I only pray that after my death, the High God will forgive me, so that I may see my friends again."

"If my conversation with her told me anything, she will forgive you."

Gil looked at the Seraph, confusion playing across his face. Ren turned her mount and rode her horse toward Tyr. She wished to discuss the change in the Divine Plane with Tyr. Now they only had one god on their side, and that might not be enough to do what needed to be done. The great owl would surely be able to give her some council.

· · ·

THAT NIGHT they made camp near a small wood. Scouts returned, saying that there were no signs of the enemy anywhere. Ren commanded that some of the trees be cut down and the wood repurposed in any way that it could. She put Gil in charge of evaluating the combat readiness of the villagers while the food was foraged and prepared. Though he made it seem as if the people of Seatown would hang him again if given the chance, what she saw told her otherwise.

In fact, it seemed like the Paladin was gathering a following of his own. At first, it seemed as if it was just those loyalists who had followed him in the burning of the fleet such as his friend Alyssa, whom he had met in Rinwaithe—but quickly it grew to be dozens more than that. Some had come around to seeing that Gil wasn't the monster that the Ten had made him out to be. Even the Admiral listened in on his training, eyeing him with less disgust than Ren would have assumed.

Ren unrolled her bedding at the edge of the small forest, sitting alone beside a fire. Divinity was hunting deeper into the trees, but the white tigress would no doubt join her shortly. The Divine Beasts hid deeper into the wood, still concerned with being spotted. Ren nearly laughed at the thought of the giant beings huddled between the trees. There was no point in staying hidden now, but old habits died hard, even among those with Divine Blood.

A lone figure walked toward the firelight, wrapped in a grey robe. One of the Balance Monks approached her, perhaps for the first time since the march had begun. Teo and Rella had kept their distance, either giving Ren her space after the loss of Trent, or simply feeling out of place now that so many followers of the Light were gathered in one place.

It was Rella who finally entered the flickering light opposite Ren. She looked as if she had been deep in thought, only returning to the world of the living to converse with the Seraph before returning to some distant plane.

"May I join you?" she asked.

"Of course," Ren said.

Rella sat down and crossed her legs. The small fire cast deep shadows across her face that melded with the swirling grey tattoos. Ren hardly knew the woman, she realized. Rella had been the Balance Monk who had aided Trent, Devin, and Gil when they had tracked a bandit blood cult to Rinwaithe in the Rim of Paradise. That same cult had killed Broderick Breaksword, a Paladin and one-time Balance Monk whom Ren had nearly thrown her life away for.

"Where is Teo?" Ren asked.

"He is meditating," Rella said slowly. "I feel like I am losing him. When this is over, I wish to restart our order. I don't know if he plans to make it that far. This quest the High God put us on is a weight that burdens him, unlike anything I have seen before."

"I'm sure that he is simply preparing his mind for the struggle to come. Has he been given any further guidance by her?"

"Not that he has told me," Rella replied. "I don't think she has spoken to him at all since before we went to the Grey Temple. You know he did what he thought was right to restore the Balance. It brought him no joy to mislead you."

"I know," Ren said, distantly. "Unlike Trent, I wasn't as shaken by his transgression. I understand your loyalty to the Balance. Once I was presented with an opportunity to follow Ravim myself. I almost took it, but I knew that I was called for something else. Did you know Broderick Breaksword when he was a Balance Monk?"

"Yes," Rella said. "He actually trained me often when I was an initiate. I was saddened when he left us to return to you."

Another friend who died under my command.

"Did you know that I saved him from being executed by my predecessor? I forfeited my life to save him, in fact. Broderick trained me as well, long before he was known as Breaksword. It was when I had rescued him that he offered for me to follow him to the Grey Temple. I stayed behind to try and kill Jerrok and prevent another purge. After becoming Seraph, I remained close with Broderick and hoped that there would be better relations between our two peoples. Though we walked different paths, we all ultimately serve the High God. Then Broderick decided the return to us, and we were blessed for a time."

Rella sat in silence for a few moments, pondering what Ren had told her. Divinity padded into the clearing and laid down between them, her white fur stained red around her mouth.

"I never told anyone this, not even Teo," she began, "but when Broderick left, I nearly followed him. I was still new to the Grey Temple at that time. My husband had been killed by bandits, and I had considered becoming a Paladin, fueled by my hatred. Instead, I went north and hoped to find peace in the mountains. I found it, and never regretted my service to the Grey God. But when Broderick left, called back to the Light one final time, I couldn't help but wonder if I had made the right choice. It wasn't vengeance that drove me that time, but a desire to protect others from suffering as I had. But I remembered that life is balance. I remembered that without my pain I never would have found peace, so I stayed.

"Later, word reached us that Broderick had been killed. That very day, the Grey God warned that the bandits responsible threatened the Balance of the world. I was chosen by Ravim himself to journey out of the temple and track them down. I was compelled to face my past as the victim of bandits, to swallow my thirst for vengeance for both my husband and now for Broderick. Only then could I restore balance. Not just for the Mortal Plane, but for myself as well."

"Did you?" Ren asked. "Did you find peace within again?"

"I did. But I discovered more than that. Just as you had with Broderick a generation before, I found friendship among the Paladins. Trent was a good man—a pained man, but good. He could have used the teachings of Ravim to spare himself from his own pain, but it was not meant to be."

Ren felt the tears welling up. She looked back into the forest.

"I did not mean to upset you," Rella said. "I simply wanted to let you know that I do understand. I have loved and lost many times in my short life." Ren could hear the other's voice cracking. "I found peace within myself thanks to the Grey God, and now even he is gone. I tried to tell this to Gil this evening, but he wouldn't listen. Vengeance will not bring you peace. It will only leave you empty. We can still seek justice for what we have lost without also losing ourselves."

Ren fought back the urge to sob. She had kept her sadness in check for the last several days, and now it came pouring out all at once. She hated herself for feeling like this. This was a weakness that she had no room for.

Rella was suddenly beside her, and she put her arm around the Seraph. A rare act of warmth from a Balance Monk. Ren placed her head on the shoulder of the other woman and finally allowed herself to cry. She noticed that Rella was crying too.

"You aren't alone, Seraph," Rella said. "I loved him too. He was a good man, and I know he loved you more than you will ever know."

"I never showed him how I felt. I mean—I did, but not enough."

"He knew."

"How do you know?" Ren asked.

"I know because I felt the same way when my husband died. And one day, we will each see our beloved again. But know this: until that day, you are not alone. The Gods of Light are falling, and the God of Balance is gone. There is only us, but that will be enough."

They sat there together until the fire burned out, and for some time after.

2

The door to his cell swung inward and two Paladins marched in. Edmund sighed and picked himself up off the floor, preparing in case they had come to beat him again. He imagined that his face was unrecognizable under the swollen black and purple lumps that likely covered it. When he was a boy, Paladins had seemed like paragons of virtue; they could do no wrong in his eyes. Now he knew the truth: they were just the same as everyone else.

The two Paladins grabbed him by the arms and dragged him from the cell. He didn't struggle. He hadn't struggled since the second day. There was no point. If he fought back, they would simply hit him harder.

Maybe that would be better.

The fatalistic part of his mind wanted them to go too far and kill him by mistake. Then this nightmare would be over. His guards had been slaughtered, and the Demigods trapped outside. There was nothing left for him outside of this cell. He only had the release of death to look forward to. He hoped that he would find peace by the High God's side.

Ajax.

He shook away the negative thoughts. He still had an oath to uphold. Two, in fact. There was an old woman and the little boy in her care that Edmund had promised to protect, and he would not shirk that vow. Somehow he would find a way back to them. There was no other choice for him to make. Elise and Ajax would survive all of this chaos, or he would die protecting them, not rotting in this cell.

The silent guards continued their walk down the hall and around the corner. They were keeping him locked in the cells beneath the Paladin barracks. He had lost track of how many days he had been down here. No one had spoken to him since the treachery at the gate. Who they were taking him to see now, he had no clue. It was possible that they finally intended to execute him. If that was the case, he would need to try and run. Somehow...

They made it to a series of stone steps. The guards allowed him to walk here, with one guard in front and one behind. The stone was cold against his bare feet. He tried not to look down at the mangled mess that remained of his toes. One of his guards liked to stomp on them when they were beating him. Edmund swallowed hard. Running would be difficult.

At the top of the stairs, they returned to dragging him until they reached the central chamber of the barracks. Edmund looked around in horror. The tapestries that had once hung from the walls were being ripped down and thrown in the center of the room. Any that showed the Gods of Light or Seraphs of old were missing. Instead, they were being replaced with banners showing various crests of the inner city families. They had finally gotten what they had wanted for hundreds of years: complete control of the city.

In the center of the great chamber was Yan and several more Paladins. As Edmund got closer, he recognized the faces of the other Paladins as well. They were the heads of some of these very families whom he had defied just days ago. None of them had been Paladins before. The old patriarchs and matriarchs held themselves above everyone else in Illux due to their Paladin lineage, but none of them had actually served the city—they had left that for their sons and daughters.

His guards came to a halt just before the group. The head of the Lighthammer family, the man called Arkon, snickered.

"Good to see you again, Captain," he said. "It has been far too long. Your chattel from the slums have been very helpful in reinforcing the barricades to the inner city. Thank you for their service."

He laughed. The others followed suit.

Edmund felt the inside of his mouth with his tongue. He found a sore that had barely healed over and bit down. Blood and pus filled his mouth. He waited as long as he could bear before spitting at Arkon. The red mess splattered Arkon's face and breastplate. The Lighthammer patriarch exploded, shouting and cursing as he knocked Edmund's guards away, grappling with the prisoner and forcing them both to the ground.

"You insolent little cur!" Arkon said through gritted teeth, his hands wrapped around Edmund's neck.

"Your nephew was a hero," Edmund choked out. "Devin Lighthammer was a champion of the people, and he gave his life for this city. You are a coward and you dishonor his name."

Arkon turned scarlet. He tightened his grip. Darkness swirled at the edges of Edmund's vision.

"Devin was a blowhard! My sister's son was no hero. He—"

"Enough!" Yan shouted.

The Paladin gripped Arkon by the cape and yanked him to his feet. Edmund sputtered and gasped, spitting more blood onto the floor. His lungs burned, but he still smiled through his cracked lips.

"The Seraph wants to see him. He's not for you to dispose of."

The Seraph?

Edmund wasn't sure that he had heard him properly. The Lady had vanished. There was no Seraph anymore. If there was, she wouldn't have allowed this blasphemy to continue. Gods be good, she would've executed each and every person in this room as a traitor as soon as she had returned to the city.

"You tell *the Seraph*," Arkon said, pointing accusingly at Yan, "that I want this little shit fed to the workers or thrown from the walls. I will not allow his attack on the honor of my house to go unanswered. Do you understand me?"

It was Yan who laughed.

"We gave you this power, and we can take it away. Don't forget that, old man," Yan said.

Edmund was picked up by his arms again and dragged from the barracks, with Yan walking in the lead. Once they were outside, Edmund could smell the smoke. He saw swirling wisps of black dotted different parts of the city skyline. Whether these came from inside or outside the walls, he wasn't sure.

"You know," Yan began, "I appreciate what you did in there. I grew up under the thumb of some of those old bastards. It's nice to see them get disrespected from time to time." He chuckled. "Can't say that Castille would approve, but *gods* it was satisfying. Devin was a little shit, though."

"He was twice the man you are," Edmund choked out.

"And now he's twice as dead. As is Trent. The Lady's lickspittles are gone, and we're what remains. You didn't even know them, not really. You didn't grow up with them. You didn't train with them. You didn't see them rise through the ranks while doing nothing to earn it. Devin got Broderick Breaksword killed, for gods' sake. They were nothing. But it was still nice to see you get old man Lighthammer all twisted up."

Edmund stayed silent, trying to ignore the barbs that Yan

threw at the men he considered friends. The Paladin was right, of course. He didn't really know either of them, and Devin even less than Trent. But his gut told him that they had been good men. Just as it had told him Tess could be trusted. It had been her who told him how Devin had been killed taking on a Divine Beast by himself. He had died a hero, there was no disputing that.

The plaza around the Grand Cathedral was mostly empty. No one trained in the practice yard, and it looked like few were coming to pray. The entire city seemed to be holding its breath waiting for something to happen. Edmund felt a little relief when he realized that the walls hadn't been breached yet. Perhaps Tess and the others had done some good out there, or that second army had overwhelmed the first. In any case, he was grateful, at least for the moment.

"How goes the siege?" he asked.

Yan merely grunted at first. "They haven't gotten in yet. Your little aberrations out there are all gone. I don't think they lasted a day."

Edmund felt sick. He had sent Tess and her people to die.

Forgive me.

They reached the steps leading into the Fourth Spire. This time he wasn't allowed to walk. One of his guards threw Edmund over his shoulder and carried him inside like he was a child. He still hadn't seen an opening to escape yet, and the prospect of doing that once he got into the Fourth Spire seemed slim. He said a silent prayer to the gods that he would be spared for at least long enough to make a break for it. He hoped they would be that foolish.

Another few minutes went by in silence as they carried him up flight after flight to the chambers of the Seraph. Edmund still wasn't sure what to think. There was no way that the Lady had returned, and yet, what other choice was there? Unless the worst had come to pass, and the gods had chosen a successor. He went cold just as the door opened and he saw his worst fears confirmed.

The Paladin threw him down at the feet of the new Seraph, Castille Denost. Edmund nearly vomited at the man's feet. The gods had indeed chosen, and poorly.

"Welcome, Edmund," Castille said, his voice stronger than it had been before.

Edmund pushed himself up to his knees. He glared at the Seraph as best he could, though he doubted any expression could be read on his swollen face. Castille smiled and offered him a hand. Edmund ignored him and stayed on his knees.

"I see you are still uncooperative," Castille murmured. "I had hoped that once you saw my divinity you would've come around."

"You're as dumb as that Lighthammer bastard," Edmund said.

Castille's face momentarily became a snarl. Then it softened again, looking almost fatherly.

"Does the choice of the gods not influence you at all? I had thought you were a pious man, at least?"

"I was," Edmund said. "I see now that perhaps my faith has been misplaced. If the Gods of Light would deign to choose such an arrogant and selfish man as you, then they don't deserve my worship, nor my respect."

The backhand that he received from Castille sent him spinning backward into the wall. He felt something in his back snap, and his leg was twisted at the wrong angle. The blow had nearly killed him. Despair washed over him as he thought of Ajax and Elise. If only he had been able to keep his mouth shut.

"Bring him to me," Castille commanded.

Edmund was dragged back to the Seraph. He cried out as the pain nearly became overwhelming. To his surprise, the Seraph kneeled down and snapped his leg back into place. A faint blue glow emanated from the winged man's hands, washing over him. Edmund felt the pain lessened and feeling return to his back and feet. Even the skin on his face seemed to loosen.

"I am not done with you yet, Captain," Castille said, standing.

"Though I will not tolerate blasphemy in my presence. When you leave here Yan, I want you to go to the wall and execute a worker. Tell them it is because of Edmund's poor choices."

"No!" Edmund shouted. "Please!"

"You need to learn consequences," Yan said, the snicker returning to his voice.

"Yes," Castille said. "Now, please don't make me hurt you again, Edmund. All I wanted was your loyalty. Redrick would have followed my every command, even before I was gifted with Divine Blood. But you? You return the gift of your station with insolence and disrespect. This rebellious attitude has passed down to most of your guards, as well. The City Watch is in open rebellion against the Paladins. They hide among the people in the slums, filling their heads with lies. I hope you can recognize how this puts the people at risk?"

Edmund nodded.

"Good. I knew that you would see some reason. If you truly care for these people, you will make these attacks against my people stop. Those traitors will be executed, of course. But the people who harbor them will not."

"How am I to speak with them?" Edmund asked, returning to his knees. "Will you let me go to them?"

Castille laughed.

"You really do think me a fool, don't you? Gods no. The next time we capture a member of the City Watch, they will be brought to you, and you can tell them what you want the others to hear. Then we will let them go spread the word. No, you will not be allowed to leave, Edmund. Not ever. Perhaps, when this is over, you can be banished from the city, if you have truly changed your ways."

"Why would you do this to your own people?"

"They need to be brought into line. Jerrok, rest his soul, knew this. Ren was weak, and a coward. She allowed the worst elements of humanity to flourish. She allowed Seatown to grow bolder than it ever has in my lifetime. She allowed us to grow feeble. Why the gods chose that traitor over me I will never know. Did you know that she attempted to assassinate Jerrok in this very room? She repressed that information after her coronation."

Edmund had heard such tales. Most he had shrugged off as lies meant to erode her rule. If what Castille said was true, it simply cemented her as the rightful ruler of this city in Edmund's eyes. She had known that power did not mean righteousness. Not in this world.

"Enough," Castille said. "Take him back to his cell. I want him brought to me tomorrow. He'll be needed for the awakening of the Guardian."

"Yes, my lord," Yan said.

"And Yan?" Castille asked.

"Don't forget to kill one of the workers for Edmund."

Yan smiled.

As they carried Edmund away, he felt despair like he had never felt before. The Gods of Light had truly abandoned their people if they had given Castille their blood. Once Ren had passed from this world, the Light had left with her. What hope did any of them have against the gods themselves?

Outside, he was returned to his feet. They allowed him to walk this time. Just as they were walking past the steps to the central chamber of the Grand Cathedral he saw a hooded woman heading inside to pray. She locked eyes with him for only a moment, her face barely visible in the shadows of her cloak. It was Liara, the woman who was most likely leading the City Watch in his absence. Her mouth formed silent words that he read on her lips: *we are coming for you.*

3

Darkness swallowed him.

It was warm and moist. A fetid stench filled his nostrils. He choked on the smell and the taste. His body howled in pain.

He knew that he was dead. He had no further strength. Nothing could save him from this destruction that enveloped him. Burning liquid splashed against his skin, melting his flesh. He screamed. The burning liquid filled his mouth.

His sword was lost. He had no weapons. No way to fight his way out.

No.

That wasn't true. He was a weapon. His blood was a weapon.

He focused the last of his strength. The liquid around him began to boil. Flames erupted from his hands, illuminating the horror around him. He was inside of the beast.

Fire shot downward. There was tearing and shuddering and blood. Everything around him shook violently.

Then he was falling.

The world rushed up to meet him. Something below came into focus. It looked like the house he had grown up in as a boy.

He punched through the roof and broke upon the floor within. His body was ruined. He would not survive what came next. Overhead, the great beast continued to shudder as the world around it was bathed in flame.

Darkness swallowed him again. But this time someone was with him. At first, he thought it was his mother. But then he knew. It couldn't be her. She was gone.

Snow was falling. His brother pushed him out of the way. Scarlet stained the ground. His hands were covered in blood.

That was who was with him now. It was his brother who dragged him to safety.

Terric had saved him again.

TRENT SLOWLY OPENED HIS EYES. The fact that every inch of his body ached was what told him that he wasn't quite dead. At least he didn't think so. He believed that there was no pain by the High God's side in the Astral Plane, in any case. Even so, he hadn't believed that he would have survived being eaten by a Divine Beast, either. All he could remember was that he had tried to blast his way out of the stomach of the creature. Whether or not that had actually been what had gotten him out, he wasn't sure.

As the world came into focus, he saw that it was nightfall. A small fire crackled in front of him. He was wrapped in blankets but was no longer wearing his armor. He looked around but couldn't see anyone else. It looked as if he was on a bed inside the remains of a small house. The roof was missing, showing the twinkling stars and the faint light of Aenna above. Trent must have still been in Seatown, but where was everyone else? Was it Ren who had saved him? Or one of the Balance Monks? For some reason, all he remembered of his savior was that they had reminded him of his brother.

He tried to sit up, but the motion made the pain overwhelming again. A cry passed his lips. He cursed himself for making so much noise before he knew exactly what was going on or who he was with. He knew better than that.

Then he saw the door open and a dark figure entered the shell of the house, carrying an armful of wood. Trent tried to see who it was, but his eyes couldn't seem to focus past the flames of the fire that danced in the center of the room.

"Thank the gods," the man said. "You're awake."

Trent felt the world drop out from under him. He recognized that voice as surely as he would recognize his own. In fact, the voice wasn't that dissimilar, for it belonged to his father. Trent leaned over the bed and heaved, though nothing came out. The man who he now knew as his father rushed to his side, to catch him. Trent recoiled from the man, clutching the blankets around himself instinctively.

"You!" Trent said. "Why are you here? What's happening?"

"Because I'm your father," the man said.

"You stopped being my father twenty years ago. I should have killed you when I had the chance!"

Trent's strength was returning, if not from his rest, then from his rage. He opened his wings, causing his father to take a step backward. The Seraph stood, looming over the man like a giant. His father cowered beneath him. Now he was the child and Trent the drunken parent, ready to land blow after blow upon his defenseless son. His hands gripped him and lifted him overhead.

"Say his name!" Trent bellowed.

"I'm sorry," his father whispered.

"Say it!"

"Terric's death was my fault!"

The image of his brother pulling him to safety flashed through his mind. He had fallen from the underbelly of Zad and landed in a house. His father had been the one to watch over him—not Terric. Terric was gone.

It can't be. This isn't possible. The High God is punishing me.

He loosened his grip, dropping his father to the ground. The pitiful man crawled away to the other side of the small fire and cowered. Trent looked down at his hands. They weren't covered in blood, but they could have been. He collapsed back onto the bed, all of his strength quickly draining. Tears formed at the corners of his eyes.

"How did this happen?" Trent asked, finally.

His father—*Brandon*, Trent tried think of him as—crawled back around the fire to face his son. His red hair was still thinning, but he had lost some weight. No doubt the road to Seatown had been filled with hardship for the man.

"I—I was out getting more supplies and," Brandon stammered.

"Start at the beginning," Trent commanded, turning so that his father couldn't see the tears in his eyes.

"After you—after I was banished, I took the road to Seatown. I figured that I had the best chance of hiding here. It seemed the least likely place that you would ever find me again. I traveled by myself the entire way and didn't see another soul. I was lucky not to have been set upon by bandits. It was as if the High God himself watched over me."

Trent snorted, but said nothing.

"I arrived at Seatown a few weeks ago. I had no money, so I was forced to beg in the streets. The Paladins mostly ignored me. I worked on their ships for a little coin. I mostly found myself thrown out of taverns once they realized I didn't have the money to shore up my tab at the end of a night of drinking. When the fleet was burned, I hid away from the mob. I wanted nothing to do with the killing, on either side. I had no plans of leaving with the people of Seatown, but I didn't care to stop them either.

"My hope was that they would leave and I could hide here, free to live out the rest of my days alone. Then you came. I saw glimpses of you and the Lady before the battle. I thought that it looked like you, but I didn't believe it until I heard her say your name. Then I knew that you had returned to me for a reason and I rushed to find you. I saw you taken inside that giant, shelled beast. Defeated, I collapsed nearly underneath it, so sure was I that my last son had been killed. But then, I saw you fall out of the belly of the thing and land in a house. I rushed to find you and pulled you to safety just as the other giant monsters destroyed that one."

Trent wiped his eyes and looked at Brandon again. His father was no longer crawling, but sitting closer to him. His expression was almost that of an expectant child, as if he hoped that Trent was going to give him the gift of forgiveness.

You're a fool, old man.

"Why did you do this?" Trent asked.

"I hated you at first, you and your friend," his father said in a measured tone. "But somewhere between here and Illux, I started to realize that there was no one to blame for my banishment besides myself. When I was younger, all I wanted was a family. When I met your mother, I thought that everything I had ever hoped for would come to pass. You boys were born soon after, and I knew that I had been blessed. Then she—" a sob stopped him for a moment, "then she died, and part of me died with her."

Now it was Trent's father who turned away to hide his tears. He took several moments to compose himself before he continued.

"Then I took to the bottle to forget her. But seeing you boys reminded me of what I had lost every day. That's no excuse, *no excuse* for what I did, mind you, but it's the truth. I hated myself for letting her die, and I hated you both for sticking around. That's why I finally kicked you out. I couldn't live with myself, let alone two living reminders of what I should have been. It's no excuse, mind you—"

"I know what it was," Trent cut him off, his anger returning. "I lived it!"

"Aye, you did, lad. I am deeply sorry for that. As I was thinking about all this on my walk here, the guilt, the true realization of what I had done settled on me like a weight that I would never be able to get out from under. By the time I reached Seatown, I wanted to jump into the ocean and let my guilt pull me to the bottom. At first I hit the bottle again, like I have always done. This time to drown even more self-loathing than when you were growing up.

"But once all of the local places started kicking me out, I was forced to sober up. And when that happened and I truly faced the horror of what I had become, of what I had done to my family," he choked up again, "to *my boys*—I decided that I needed to do something, anything to make it right. I was going to live here—alone, like I mentioned—in some self-imposed exile, while I figured out what that something would be. But then, the High God dropped you back into my lap and gave me a second chance."

"You don't deserve it," Trent growled.

"No, you're right," Brandon said. "I don't deserve it, but *you do*."

"What?"

"My pain has become your pain, son. My abuse, my anger, my *evil*—it has all become your burden to bear, and it weighs you down. I have only seen you twice since you were a boy, and both times you have tried to kill me. I deserve no less, but I can see it in your eyes, you can't let go of your hate for me any more than I can. And if there is one thing I am going to do, it is free you, son."

Suddenly, Brandon stood. Some backbone had seemed to return to Trent's father, or else the man had lied about cutting off the liquid courage. He rustled through a bundle of rags to the side of the bed and pulled out a giant sword. Trent's breath caught in his throat as he recognized Godtaker.

"I found it in the ruins just below where you fell," his father said, handing him the weapon. "I can't ask you to forgive me, son. I don't deserve that. But I ask that you let your anger go. Don't let me hold you back any longer."

Brandon grabbed the tip of the blade and pressed it into his chest.

"If you need to end it this way, then so be it. Otherwise, I will leave you and go to the north, seek out the Grey Temple."

Trent saw resolution in his father's eyes. The old man was serious. He would live or die to please his son. There was no fear there, only sadness and regret. Trent pictured the sight of Terric falling in the snow. The smell of his blood once again filled his nostrils. He gripped Godtaker and pushed the point deeper into his father's chest. He had waited his entire life for this moment. Justice would finally be his, and he would be at peace.

Terric's choice isn't something that you should blame yourself for. He doesn't blame you. I promise he would do it again.

The High God's words echoed in his memory. If Terric didn't blame Trent for his death, did he blame Brandon? If their father hadn't kicked them out on the street then he would be alive, wouldn't he? Or would they have always found their way to that Demon? No matter where they had been living, they would have still seen the smoke and been curious.

His hands loosened. Terric had chosen to be selfless and save his brother. Trent would not dishonor him by doing this. He would do as Terric had done, and chose life. Godtaker fell to the floor with a resounding crash. The Seraph grabbed his father and embraced him. Both men cried openly now.

"I'm so sorry," his father said.

"I know," Trent replied. "I know."

"Forgive me."

"I will try, for my brother if no one else."

THE NEXT MORNING, while his father looked for breakfast, Trent put his armor back on. He felt the tightness in his face and was reminded of the damage that he had sustained from the venom of that Divine Beast. His father had told him that the others had left with the people of Seatown behind them. He assumed that they marched for Illux. Trent would have little time to catch up to them before it was too late. Though he spared him some of the details, Trent had also filled in his father on what he had been through that had made him a Seraph and led him to battle giant monsters in Seatown.

He longed for Ren, to hold her again and tell her what had transpired here. No doubt she and the others thought that he was dead. That saddened him, for he knew what he would be like if he thought Ren had died. Yet here he was. Since deciding to spare his father the night before, Trent felt more at peace than he had in his entire life. Even with the threat of death still looming over him, he knew that he was more whole than he had been the day before.

His father returned with some scraps of food that he had scavenged from one of the taverns. They ate in relative silence, the cawing of gulls returning after the activity of the last few days scared them farther down the coast.

"I want to come with you," his father said.

"For what purpose?" Trent asked. "I travel to a battle the likes of which the Mortal Plane hasn't seen in a thousand years. That is no place for you, father."

"I don't care. I would follow you to Infernaak itself. I won't leave you again. This is my penance. If I die protecting you, so be it."

"So be it," Trent said.

By late morning, the Seraph was flying west, carrying his father in his arms.

4

His kingdom stretched out beneath him from where he sat high atop his throne. For the first time in a thousand years, he no longer felt like the Fallen One. He was Lio, God of Light, once more. Below the throne that had once belonged to the High God, Luna stood, looking into the Basin of Aenna, watching the siege that would soon overtake Illux. Though he did not know it, the Seraph Castille served Lio now, and his every action served to further his plans. If Illux held off the siege, then the Light would still be under his thrall, and soon, even they would face oblivion.

And our new servants will rise.

Lio stood and walked down the steps to stand beside his new companion. He sized her up as he made his way down to her. Her loyalty to him had come as a complete shock those few days ago. If it had not been for her timely intervention, Lio would have died as the Fallen One, killed by the Gods of Darkness. He had overestimated his ability to keep them groveling at his feet. He would not make that mistake again.

"Tell me," he said, his voice honey, "why has it taken you until now to come to my aid? I have suffered a millennium as the Fallen One, and not once did you even speak to me as an equal."

She paused, looking up from the Basin. Deep regret blossomed behind her eyes.

"Forgive me," she said. "I was too weak. I didn't dare to cross the others. Arra, Samson, Ravim. I was afraid that if I reached out to you in any way, I would be lost. But I never, *never*, stopped loving you."

The goddess walked up and stroked the scar across his face. He tried not to recoil in revulsion. She could never replace Daniel. No matter what she thought.

Has she truly always felt like this? Why can't I remember?

He tried to wrack his brain, thinking back to the last time he was just Lio, back before he was cast down. He had been fast friends with all of the Gods of Light, but he had never loved them like he had loved Arra—and even that was only as a sister. No, he did not remember Luna ever showing him attention in that way. He only ever had eyes for a mortal man...

Lio clenched his fists. Startled, Luna stepped back, afraid that he would lash out at her. Once he saw that she still recognized his power he relaxed his grip. He couldn't lose her as an ally, not yet. Not while two other gods still stood against him.

"Do not be afraid," he cooed. "I am eternally grateful for your...loyalty. I promise that it will be rewarded in time. For now, I can't bear to give my heart to another, not until this is done."

"Yes, of course. I overstepped. But I knew! I knew that you would always be a God of Light. The others, they were weak. But not you. You were the one who killed Xyxax. You were the only one of us who was truly strong. I—we all betrayed you."

Her eyes fell downward. Lio tried to read her. There was something that she wasn't telling him. Something that chewed at the edges of her mind. No matter—he would learn everything from her in time, and once she had no more secrets to tell, he would become the only God of Light.

"How is our new Seraph?" he asked, looking into the Basin himself.

"He does well," her voice returned to its normal lyrical tones. "Castille has nearly crushed his opposition within the city. He will soon awaken the Guardian, and after that..."

"Before the city falls, he will begin the creation of our new army," Lio finished. "An army that will never fall, that will never betray us."

"What of your *monsters?*" she asked, the last word sticking in her mouth.

"They have almost served their purpose. Once they have finished dealing with the traitors, they will sack Illux and wipe it clean. After that, I will finish them myself. But first," he paused, breaking the surface of the silver liquid with his fingers, "we will need to finish Samson and Rhenaris. The Mortal and Divine Planes will be ours, all at once."

The surface of the Basin shimmered; the smoke and carnage of Illux were replaced with the dusty plains of the south. Lio was searching, casting his gaze through the window to the Mortal Plane in a frenzied attempt to find his quarry. He stood there in silence, ignoring the presence of the goddess until he finally found what he was looking for.

"Leave me," he commanded.

"Where shall I—" she began.

"I don't care!" he snapped.

The goddess turned and slinked away, sulking like a struck dog. He would never love her. Not like he had loved Daniel.

Daniel, my love.

Below him, the former Seraph was making his way across the southern plains, heading for the spiked ruins that had been Godsend. Lio gripped the edges of the Basin, the stone groaning between his fingers. He leaned in, his nose nearly touching the silver blood.

Daniel, answer me. Please.

The grey warrior didn't stop. His pace was relentless, his countenance grim. The warrior had survived his showdown with that wretched woman Ren, but he had not returned to Lio's other forces. With Merek dead, Lio feared that he would lose Daniel too.

Please. Why don't you answer me?

Merek had never lost sight of their cause, even knowing what lengths Lio needed to go to become the lone God of Light. But Daniel had been driven mad by the cruel torture of Xyxax. What was left of his mind, Lio didn't know. Perhaps he was truly a monster now, no different from the Demons who assaulted Illux or the Herald who led them.

I will come to you, then.

Lio leaned into the surface of the Basin, the rush of the silver blood filling his nose and mouth.

Don't.

Lio pulled his head back from the surface as if he had been struck. Daniel didn't sound like himself. He didn't sound like Lio had remembered him. It wasn't possible.

Why? Don't you love me? We can be together again. I've done all of this for you. Don't you see that?

The words in his mind spilled out of him like he was a madman. He could feel his grip on his sanity slipping. The same feeling of despair that had overtaken him these last thousand years was returning.

"No, no, no" he muttered aloud.

You are the Nightbreaker. I am the God of Light. We are one.

Finally, the small grey figure stopped running. For a moment, Daniel seemed to be looking straight into Lio's eyes through Aenna on the Plane below. The god reached his hand out to touch the surface again.

No. I am the Nightbringer now. And you are nothing more than the shell of a god. Kill me if you must, but never speak to me again.

Lio's hands struck the surface of the Basin with such force that silver blood rained onto the throne behind him. He spun facing the only other object of his desire beside the man who had just scorned him. He screamed loud enough that surely Luna would think he was in danger. His fists struck the High God's throne again and again. The stone crumbled into rubble beneath him. He screamed and tore at his face between attacks. When it was finished, he was kneeling in the pile of stone that had once looked over all of creation.

Luna returned to him, tears in her eyes. No doubt he was covered in Divine Blood, some from the Basin, some from his ruined hands. She knelt beside him, checking him for further injury.

"What happened?" she asked. "What's wrong?"

"Tell Castille to accelerate our plans," he whispered. "I want the Mortal Plane cleansed within the week."

She nodded and stood, walking back to the Basin. In moments, she was gone, traveling below to talk with their newest servant. He kneeled there, alone, for what seemed to be hours. When the Fallen One finally stood, Lio was well and truly dead.

5

"Why?" the trembling man whispered.

He was hanging upside-down from the chandelier above his ornate dinner table. Drops of blood ran down his face from the cut on his chin, dripping melodically onto a silver platter below him. His wife and two children were tied up against the wall. They were all gagged and the children were blindfolded. They whimpered pitifully but quietly to not draw the attention of the man who stood in front of their father.

Arkos Lighthammer examined the point of his sword in a non-interested way. He looked much like his cousin Devin, with dark skin and a tight beard. His Paladin armor was marked with droplets of blood from his earlier confrontation with his victim. This wasn't the first time he had done this and, High God willing, it wouldn't be the last.

"Did you say something?" he asked, looking back up at the man.

"Why are you doing this? You of all people?" The man asked again.

"Careful. I can't have your children hear my name, or I will have to kill them too," Arkos lied.

He drew the line at children. He had become a killer, but he was no monster.

Or am I? What would Devin think of me?

He tried not to think of his cousin at moments like this. Especially now that it sounded like Devin and Trent had died with the Lady Ren. Arkos dishonored him, but this was the only way that he knew how to truly serve the Light anymore.

"Do you really not know why?" Arkos asked.

The man's wife began to wail through her gag.

"You have abused the people of the slums, time and time again. And your crimes don't stop there…"

Arkos trailed off. It had been several years since he had done this regularly. Early on, he had nearly been caught by the City Watch. Self-preservation had made him ignore his desire to clean up the inner city of its corruption. The madness of the siege had given him an opportunity that he couldn't pass up.

"We never hurt anyone!" the man spat.

"Liar!" Arkos shouted.

The Paladin pricked the man's chest with the sword. His first kill he had been filled with rage, as much of an attack on his father as it had been on that Silvershield rapist. He tried not to let his anger control *these* killings. This was justice.

"You are known to beat your servants from the slums. As is your wife."

"What inner city family doesn't instill some discipline in their workers? I always paid them well."

"Aye," Arkos said. "And what was the phrase you told me once over dinner here? The knowledge goes in where the blood comes out?"

Arkos struck the man across the face with the back of his hand.

"Well, I expect you to learn quite a bit today then. No, that is not the worst of your crimes. What of the girl, Iliriel?"

The man paled.

"I-I-I," he stammered.

"You had an affair with her. She was still a child herself when you impregnated her, wasn't she?"

"She was a grown woman!"

Arkos struck him again. This time, it had been too hard and the man hung there limp. The Paladin picked up the woman and slammed her on the table. He pulled the gag from her mouth.

"And you killed her, didn't you?" he hissed.

"What are you talking about?" she cried.

"You were embarrassed and jealous and angry, weren't you?"

"Yes, but I didn't hurt the wretch," she proclaimed. "It was all Arthur. It was just my husband. Please, let me and my girls go."

Arkos grabbed her by the cheeks and squeezed hard. Droplets of her husband's blood started to land on her face, mingling with her tears.

"Tell me the truth and I will spare the children," he said.

"Yes!" she shouted. "I killed her. I beat her to death with the rod we used to discipline them. I couldn't stand the thought of her raising his little bastard, here or in the slums. Arthur helped me get rid of her body! How did you know that?"

"Walls talk in this city. Rumors spread quickly, and, unlike others, I listen."

"Please! Let me go with my girls! We will leave Illux! I swear!"

Arkos laughed at this. "And how would you possibly do that? We are under siege, woman."

"Several families are planning to use a secret passage through the catacombs that leads to the outside of the wall. We were planning to flee once the outer wall is breached and the Forces of Darkness are distracted by the slums."

Does he know?

Arkos turned and looked away from the woman, his rage building. This disgusted him almost more than the crimes this family had committed. He knew that Castille and his father would prioritize the protection of the inner city families over that of the people in the slums. But using their deaths as a distraction while they flee like cowards? Where was their pretend honor in that?

"You have been found guilty of abuse and murder," Arkos said quietly. "I will now mete out your punishment."

"Please!" the woman screamed.

ANOTHER MANOR BURNING wasn't out of the ordinary during these trying times. Likely, it would be blamed on the City Watch members still loyal to Edmund. The family he had killed wasn't powerful enough for Castille to waste resources looking much deeper than that.

Arkos continued on his walk back to the Lighthammer Manor lost in his thoughts. He had spared the two girls, leaving them with a group of refugees in the slums. They never saw his face or heard his name. No one would come looking for them in the slums, so there was no chance he would be found out. Not that it mattered if he was. By his reckoning, he only had a few more days to live in any case. Then, he could meet his cousin again by the High God's side.

The blinding light of the midday sun nearly obscured Aenna completely. The opening to the Divine Plane had grown so faint over the last few weeks that Arkos half-expected it to disappear completely. He wasn't sure how he felt about that. All that drove him these days was a desire to punish those of Illux's upper class who expected to get away with their crimes now that one of their own was Seraph again.

Castille.

The fact that the Gods of Light had made that corrupt fool the next Seraph disgusted Arkos. Long had he chafed under the rule of his father and Castille. They truly thought themselves better than the poorer citizens of Illux. They looked down on men like Trent, even on men like Devin, who called them friends. Once, Arkos had been weak like that. Then he had woken up.

The grounds of his family home rose to meet him. Little comfort that it was to be under the same roof as his father, he figured that he didn't feel as exposed there as he did walking the streets after the killing.

The Paladin shoved open the great doors to the entrance chamber and continued on, ignoring the gasps from the servants that he passed. No doubt they were taken aback by the blood that covered his white breastplate. With the chaos engulfing the city these last few days, he could explain it away as belonging to a rebel and not arouse a second thought.

In the great hall, he saw the fabled Lighthammer hanging above the hearth. Even though Castille had finally made Arkos's father a Paladin, the old man still had the good sense to leave the hammer be. It hadn't been removed since it was used by Arkos to slay Julius Silvershield.

"Where have you been?" Arkon Lighthammer asked, looking up from a schematic he had on the table in front of him.

"Patrolling the city," Arkos lied.

His father looked him up and down but said nothing, though fear did flash in his eyes. Arkos knew that his father had often suspected him of the killings that occurred in the inner city, but his own concern with appearance kept his lips sealed.

"Yes, very good," Arkon trailed off. "You are needed in the cata-combs. The Seraph has a special project taking place there.

"Is this the plan to run like cowards I have heard rumor of?"

Arkon looked around quickly before moving closer to his son. His face contorted into anger as he spoke next.

'Where did you hear that?" he whispered.

"As I said, father, rumors," Arkos replied.

"Well," Arkos said, his false confidence returning, "you best keep rumors such as that to yourself. We don't want the Seraph to hear of such things. No, Castille says that the goddess has given him a plan that will help save the city. Maybe then we won't need…alternatives."

It's your plan, then. I should have known—even as a Paladin, you are the most self-serving coward in this city.

"When am I needed below?" Arkos asked.

"Now."

6

Things are not going well for Illux.

Samson's voice was weaker than it had been before. He didn't sound as if he was recovering from the injuries that Luna had dealt him. While she still technically served him, Ren had begun to doubt the efficacy of the Gods of Light or, more accurately, the last God of Light. After all, Samson had allowed himself to be betrayed, and he had doubted Trent. What was he now besides a false ideal that hid in Ayyslid, waiting for it all to be over?

How do you know? Have you been to the Basin?

No. But the prayers of the righteous have filtered up to my ears. They are afraid. Many of them are already dying.

What would you have me do?

Come to their aid! How close are you? I fear they don't have more than a few days.

Ren looked ahead at the miles of grassland and rolling hills. She knew that he spoke the truth. At the rate her army was going, they wouldn't reach the city in time. Not unless she could provide Illux with a way to hold off the horde for another few days at least. Still, she knew what she must do.

The army isn't close enough, but I have a plan.

What?

It doesn't matter. It will work. It has to.

She could feel the god seething from above. Even in his weakened state, he didn't like being talked to like they were equals. It didn't matter, not anymore. Either way, Ren couldn't risk Luna listening to her thoughts as they filtered up to Samson. She had no way of knowing if her attempts at talking only to him were working or not. Until now, she never had a reason to hide anything from any of her gods.

Your insolence—

My insolence may yet keep you alive. Though I doubt you deserve even that.

She could feel Samson's mind recoil from hers as if he had been struck. Ren clenched her fists, drawing the attention of her riding companions. Vaguely, she was aware that Rella reached out for her, but the woman's hand was stayed by Teo.

You would dare to speak to me this way? I am your god!

You are a coward and a weakling who couldn't sniff out the treachery under his very nose. The only one of you who was worth a damn was Arra, and you let her die! Now you hide in Ayyslid like a scared child, awaiting his mommy to save him from the monsters. You don't command me anymore, Samson. I will ask your counsel when I deign to, and that is all. Keep yourself alive long enough for us to break the siege, so that the Paladins don't lose their strength. Beyond that, expect nothing more from your people.

The wounded god remained silent, though his anger did seem to soften. To Ren, it felt like it was replaced with sadness. She had truly isolated him now, and that, no doubt, cut deeper than Luna's blade.

The Seraph blinked and looked around. She realized that she

had stopped riding during her tirade against Samson. The army had stopped marching and all eyes were now on her. Ren shook her head and started her horse forward again.

"Well?" Rella prodded, against Teo's protestations. "What did he say?"

"We are alone now, as you said," Ren replied. "The strength of the last God of Light has failed, and I won't allow him to pull us down with him."

"What do you mean?" Gil asked, breaking his silence.

"Samson hides in Ayyslid like a wounded dog, and yet he still thinks that he can bark orders to us down here. We can rely on his counsel no longer. I will close my mind off to him unless I have no other choice. What happens to our people falls to us now."

Ren thought back to her own time as a Paladin, when her confidence in the wisdom of her Seraph had likewise faltered. She had taken matters into her own hands then as well.

And look how that turned out.

The earth shook slightly as the massive form of Tyr landed beside them. Ren could feel the anger radiating off of the Divine Beast. She nearly shivered. No doubt Samson had begun speaking to the other bearers of Divine Blood to turn them against her. Was this really what it had come to? The Light was going to fall because it sought to destroy itself.

"Tyr—" she began.

"My lady," he interrupted, his voice shaking the ground. "If I may." Ren nodded. "If only my blood would allow it, I would fly through Aenna and lay waste to Ayyslid myself."

Ren almost stopped her horse again, she was so taken aback. Dumbfounded, she couldn't find any words, so she nodded again.

"You are our only leader now. I speak for the others when I say that we are ashamed at how far the Light has fallen. First the treachery of Luna, and now Samson would dare to question you! He spoke to us, telling us each that you were challenging his authority and choosing to ignore his council. If that is so, then you have your reasons and we will not question them. My lady, if any can lead us to victory—"

"That's enough, Tyr," Ren said. "I appreciate your counsel and, most of all, your loyalty. This isn't how I wanted this to happen, but I have no choice. The Mortal Plane stands alone, perhaps for the better. Regardless, Samson did share something with me. The prayers of Illux grow more frantic by the day, and the people have begun dying. They cannot wait for us to arrive with the full might of the army. We have to slow down the siege and buy them more time."

"What did you have in mind?" the Divine Beast asked.

"I want you and the others to fly ahead to the city so that we can hold them off long enough for us to get there. Can those who cannot fly manage this?"

"We will find a way."

"Good. The Balance Monks and I will accompany you as well."

Ren noticed that Teo cracked a faint smile. Rella nodded her approval. It was stoic Gil who raised a protest.

"My lady," he began shakily. "If you leave, what will keep the Admiral from turning her people around and marching back to the sea? Send the Divine Beasts ahead, yes, but don't leave the army without a true leader."

"Admiral Wyn strikes me as a woman of her word," Ren said, looking back at the green-blue cloak of the woman riding just out of earshot behind them. "I don't think that she will abandon us. Not yet. Besides, I am not leaving them alone. I am leaving them with *you.*"

Gil's face, which until now had been a mask of unbreakable determination, grew flush and his eyes fell.

"My lady, I cannot. I killed many of these people in my quest to keep them from fleeing. They bear no love for me."

"This is your penance, then. I charge you not just with bringing them to Illux's aid, but with their safety as well. These people are your charges, Gil. It's up to you to make sure that they are not left to die if saving Illux cannot be done." Ren turned to look away from the bewildered Paladin, but a flash of green from behind her reminded her of something. "And one more thing. The sack over your head prevented you from seeing who it was that actually cut you out of that noose. Perhaps the Admiral forgives you more than you would assume."

Gil nodded and allowed his horse to fall behind.

"We will continue on with the others until nightfall," Ren said. "Once camp is made, I will inform the Admiral of our plan and we will depart."

THAT NIGHT, the army made camp in a small valley, nestled between two low-sloping hills. In the distance, a crumbling tower cut a dark line through the orange and pink sky. A remnant of a time when the Forces of Light were united in purpose and actually did what was right.

When two villagers came to pitch a tent for the Seraph to sleep in, she waved them off. They left looking confused. It didn't take long for Wyn to find Ren after that, her face a shade darker as she chewed on her lip. The Admiral was flanked by two guards. In the distance, Ren saw Gil sulking around, his downcast eyes locked onto the other woman. For all of his claims that she was a good woman, he was still afraid that she couldn't be trusted, it seemed. Perhaps he no longer held confidence in his own judgment.

"I heard that you chose not to have a tent this night," Wyn said. "Do you wish to admire the night sky, or are you planning on leaving us? What was it that the Gods of Light told you that you didn't share with the rest of us?"

Ren had chosen to keep Luna's treachery from becoming common knowledge, lest the tenuous alliance between her and

Seatown crumble completely without their shared faith to bind them.

"Illux cannot hold for much longer. The Divine Beasts and I will go on ahead to help hold the city until the rest of you arrive."

Wyn's expression hardened.

"I say again that we are no army. If Illux is falling that quickly, we will do nothing to help besides prolonging its demise. I implore you, allow us to turn back if victory is unobtainable. Please."

Ren reached out and placed her hand on the Admiral's shoulder.

"If Illux cannot be saved, I don't expect your people to die for it. Continue on to the city and decide for yourself once you see the siege. If we haven't made an impact by then, take your people and return to the sea. Sail away from here and try to find safety somewhere far to the east."

"Damn you," Wyn said, a light smirk forming, "I wish my father were here. He wouldn't have allowed the fear of what was best for his people to keep him up like this."

"If he was as good a leader as you say, he would have."

Wyn nodded and turned around, walking back into camp. As she passed Gil his eyes fell again. She stopped and said something that Ren couldn't hear. The one-armed Paladin fell into line behind her and followed her back to the others.

Teo, Rella, and Divinity emerged from the growing shadows. Behind them, the hulking shapes of the Divine Beasts blocked out the shape of the crumbling tower. They were united at least, and that would have to be enough.

"It's time."

7

We are coming for you.

Liara spoke to Edmund, her mouth moving but making no sound. Her hand reached out for his. He tried to grab her but couldn't quite reach. Yan was holding him back. He struggled.

Edmund punched the Paladin, shrugging him off. He reached out again. A silver sword severed his arm at the elbow. A gout of steaming red sprayed Liara's face. She fell away, screaming as her skin began to smoke. Dumbly, Edmund looked up to see who had swung the blade. It had been a silver corpse.

A SHARP KICK brought Edmund awake. He could feel the sickly sweat that covered his body. Liara had not come for him, not yet. He sucked in air and clutched at his bruised ribs. Yan was standing over him, his usual menace replaced by some shade of pity.

"Get up," he chided. "Bad dreams, eh?"

"Better than waking," Edmund lied.

The Paladin chuckled.

"I'll tell you what," Yan said, "you come along quietly, and I'll make sure you return to your dream world unmolested tonight. Sound fair?"

"Sounds like a load of shit," Edmund said, taking the Paladin's outstretched hand.

Yan's smirk left. Edmund walked to the corner and pissed in the bucket they had given him. When he was done, he followed Yan out the door and into the hallway. To his surprise, the Paladin didn't grab him and drag him this time. Perhaps Yan trusted him to truly come quietly. Edmund's thoughts drifted back to Liara.

His mistake.

They exited the barracks and walked toward the Cathedral, just like the day before. Edmund wasn't sure if he was being taken back to see Castille again. All he knew was that he was needed to awaken the Guardian. What that entailed he would rather not guess. In any case, he was just relieved that he wasn't being dragged to his destination again.

His eyes flitted around the plaza, looking for anyone that seemed out of place. He hoped that Liara would choose this moment to strike. Yan was his only guard at this moment. This lapse in judgment could be the only chance the guards had to save him. All he saw were normal inner city citizens going about their business as if the world outside wasn't burning down around them. To add to this dichotomy, Edmund saw plumes of smoke swirling on the horizon. He ground his teeth as he thought about the people in the slums being forced to work to protect the cowards in here...

"Did you do it?" Edmund heard himself asking, against his better judgment.

"What?" Yan asked.

"Kill one of the workers?" His fists were already clenching.

"Of course," Yan said. "I always follow orders."

Edmund you idiot.

Edmund jumped onto the back of the Paladin, raking his face with the claw-like nails on his ragged fingers. Yan howled and reached up to pull him off, but not before Edmund bit down on Yan's left ear. Blood filled his mouth as the flesh ripped away from the Paladin's head. Edmund went spinning through the air and landed on the ground with a wet crunch. There went one of his ribs.

Yan cursed and stumbled after him, catching Edmund across the face with his boot. The world spun into darkness as Edmund tumbled back to the ground. His thoughts refused to coalesce into anything besides the recognition of pain for the next several moments. When he finally came to, he was slung over the blood-covered shoulder of the Paladin. It took him a while to realize that his eyes were indeed open again, as he was now in a dark stairwell. They must have been returning to the upper levels of the Fourth Spire to visit Castille. Then he noticed that they were headed down, not up.

Gods have mercy.

They were going down to the catacombs.

Edmund tried to wrack his brain to figure out just what Castille had planned down here. The catacombs stretched from the Grand Cathedral to the walls, spider-webbing under the city in a maze of tunnels and chambers. Originally the catacombs were built to house the dead from the Northern Campaign, but soon they grew to be the only resting place of those who died in Illux. At one time, entrances existed all over the city, to allow easy access to visit deceased loved ones, as well as to provide escape routes in case the city was breached. Now, however, almost all of those locations had been sealed or lost, leaving only the entrances under the cathedral in operation.

The stairs vanished as Yan carried Edmund out onto a large landing. The air down here was stale and musty from a thousand years of decay. Edmund shivered in spite of himself. He had only been below ground a few times in his life, and he hated it. Already his lungs screamed for the air of the surface, and he fought to keep his fear in check. Distant voices broke the deathly silence of the hall as Yan continued on in silence.

After a long period of time walking past alcoves filled with corpses, they found themselves in a larger central chamber. It was a giant circle, with passages shooting off in every conceivable direction. Dozens of torches had been lit in the place to allow the most light possible. Yan dropped Edmund onto the ground in the center of the chamber.

"My lord," the Paladin said from behind Edmund.

The Captain of the City Watch sat upright, looking in awe at the number of people gathered down here. Dozens of carts were being wheeled down the passages, manned by Paladins and refugees alike. Those that returned to the central chambers were filled with armored corpses in various states of decay.

"What in the High God's name is happening?" Edmund whispered under his breath.

He saw that Castille stood off to the side, overseeing the excavation of Illux's fallen. Yan approached the Seraph cautiously, visibly shaken for the first time that Edmund had ever seen. Even he knew that whatever was happening down here wasn't right.

"Ah, Yan," Castille said as if noticing him for the first time. "What happened to your face?"

The Paladin nodded at Edmund. In the torchlight, it seemed as if he had been mauled by a bear. Edmund smiled, though he wondered why the Paladin hadn't healed himself.

Castille reached out and touched Yan's face, his hand glowing bright blue. The deep cuts mended and vanished, though his ear didn't grow back. Once he was done, the Seraph turned and grabbed the arm of another Paladin who was pushing a cart deeper into the catacombs.

"As I said, prepare the others for what is about to happen. We don't want anyone to fall in. I want the corpses deposited near the practice field. Start gathering all of the steel that isn't currently in the hands of a Paladin."

"My lord," the Paladin said, visibly shaken. "Some of the others are afraid that we risk the wrath of the gods by disturbing the dead. If they knew—"

"The wrath of the gods?" Castille's laugh filled the chamber. "The gods are the ones who have ordered this. The goddess has promised me that what we do today will ensure that the inner city is protected from any advance. Now, gather the *steel.*"

"My lord." The Paladin nodded and scurried off.

One of the carts brushed Edmund's side. He looked up just in time to see the flash of a familiar face. Liara was taking an empty cart down one of the hallways. A hand hung over the side of her cart—a hand that was not decayed in the slightest.

The seraph walked over to Edmund then, picking the man up by the front of his shirt.

"You disappoint me, Captain," he said. "I thought you learned yesterday that resistance only hurts those you claim to protect. How many need to die to sustain your vanity, hmm?"

"I wasn't resisting, *my lord,* I was simply paying Yan back for the life he took yesterday."

Castille chuckled and set Edmund back down.

"I can't say you improved his appearance. Now then, let's get on with the next command of the goddess."

Castille drew his sword and struck Edmund across the chest. The cut was long, but not deep. Blood seeped from Edmund's shoulder to his waist. His skin burned with cold fire as he slumped to the floor. As he lay there, he realized that the ground wasn't paved stone here, but perfectly smooth, and it soaked up his blood with a wicked thirst. Yan and several other Paladins pricked his arms and legs with their own blades, before walking to the edges of the circle and stabbing them into the floor.

What is happening?

Edmund felt weak. His strength was draining from the myriad of small wounds. Rough hands grabbed him and dragged him to the edge of the circle. He saw a faint blue glow from the edges of his vision as the various cuts began to mend. Looking up, Edmund saw that it was Yan who was healing him. But why?

Suddenly, Castille took to the air, flying to the zenith of the vaulted ceiling in the chamber, his hand glowing with blue light. All at once, every torch in the chamber went out as if some wind had blown down from the surface. Everything plunged into blackness save for the hands of the Seraph.

Blue energy slammed into the buried sword blades. The earth shook violently, causing shadowy stones to fall from the ceiling. The rumbling continued until Edmund was sure that the Seraph had gone completely mad and was going to bring the entire cathedral down onto their heads. Yan clutched Edmund's arm tighter.

Then the shaking stopped.

The torches began producing light again. It seemed as though they hadn't been blown out after all. Edmund looked around to see if anything else had changed. Standing in the tunnel directly across from him, he saw Liara and a dozen other faces he recognized with the glint of steel in their hands.

We are coming for you.

Then a thunderous crack filled the chamber, echoing down every hall. Then another, and another. No one else noticed the guards preparing to strike, for all eyes were cast to the center of the smooth circle, which was now crisscrossed with jagged lines. All at once, the floor in the center of the chamber fell away into an impossibly deep pit. The light of torches refused to illuminate what was inside.

"Guardian!" Castille shouted. "You have been summoned by the Goddess Luna to defend your city! Illux is under siege, the Pact has been broken and mind of Samson lost. We need you now, in our darkest hour. Be free of the prison the Grey God chained you to. Save our city!"

All held their breath.

"As the goddess commands," a deep voice rumbled from within the pit.

An impossibly large shape emerged from the pit at lightning speed. Castille quickly darted to the side as the behemoth smashed through the ceiling, flooding the chamber with light. As the stones of the catacombs rained down around them, Edmund caught a glimpse of the winged creature. It had the body of a great cat, but the head of an eagle. The Seraph had summoned his own Divine Beast.

Then several things happened at once:

Castille flew out of the chamber into the grey sky above, following behind the Guardian. Several large stones fell, knocking a few Paladins and workers who were too close to the edge into the pit. Yan relaxed his grip on Edmund as the quarrel of a crossbow bolt sprouted from his chest. Liara and her guards rushed around the edges of the pit, cutting down as many unaware Paladins as they could.

Edmund was still too weak to fight back but was able to roll away from the stunned Paladin just as Liara reached them. Her blade struck Yan across the arm. The injured Paladin fell back into one of the tunnels where he began groping for a rusty blade among the dead. Liara pulled Edmund to his feet and led him to one of the passages. Edmund was so turned around that he wasn't sure if they were headed back to the Cathedral or deeper into the tombs.

The sounds of battle behind them told him that it probably didn't make a difference.

8

The catacombs continued on endlessly in front of them. The mocking faces of the dead leered out of their alcoves where they slumbered, staring at Edmund with their empty eyes. Shadows danced around the decaying bodies from Liara's torch. The sounds of the battle had begun to fade in the distance behind them. Liara stopped at a junction, looking left and then right.

"Do you know where you're going?" Edmund rasped.

"Why don't you turn around, run headlong back into that hole and then—" Liara started, a smile forming.

"Point taken," Edmund said as they started to the left.

It was then that Edmund realized he was unarmed. He stopped for a moment and pried an old sword from the hands of a skeletal warrior. Thank the gods that they were in a Paladin wing of the catacombs. As they continued down the hall, Edmund's mind raced. Castille had a Divine Beast doing his bidding. It wasn't just the Darkness that had those creatures anymore! But it was still only his enemies. And what had they been doing with the bodies of the dead? What had the goddess Luna promised them?

And what can we do to stop it?

They turned another corner and nearly ran into another member of the City Watch. It was a short, squat man called Hubert. Hubert almost gutted Edmund before skittering to a halt. When he recognized Edmund his eyes lit up with excitement. His sword returned to its sheath and he stood at attention.

"Sir!" Hubert said.

Edmund said nothing and hugged the man. Behind them, Liara grunted. Laughing, Edmund turned and hugged her too. The silence of the dead around them was deafening.

"How in the High God's name did you find me?" Edmund asked.

"By accident, sir," Liara said, matter-of-factly. "We had no idea you would be down here. In fact, we were watching the plaza, waiting for a moment to ambush Yan and the other Paladins to bust you out. But then they started taking workers this morning and dragging them down here. I decided that we leave you for the time being and see what Castille was doing inside the cathedral. It was just dumb luck that you were here."

"It wasn't luck," Edmund said. "It was providence."

"Yes," Hubert said. "The Gods of Light smile on us."

"No," Edmund said. "The Gods of Light chose Castille. They have forsaken us. But the High God has not. He brought us back together, and he will get us out of here."

Or I will.

Edmund walked past Hubert back the way the guard had come, following the hallway until it turned again. They continued on this path for what felt like hours until finally, Edmund reached a dead end. The alcoves here were crumbling, the corpses barely more than dust in rusted armor. The wall at the end though, had no corpses.

He ran his fingers over the stone. It was smoother than the

stone of the alcoves, and it looked relatively newer. Edmund knocked on the wall with the pommel of his sword in multiple places. The wall was hollow.

"This is it!" Edmund hissed, "This is one of the exits. This wall was placed here to stop criminals from hiding beneath Illux. This happened to several of the entrances to the catacombs after the Paladins caught a murderer who was using these passages to move about the city. We just need to break through."

The Captain of the City Watch struck the wall with his sword as hard as he could. A small piece of stone crumbled and fell to the ground. He raised his hand again, but Liara stopped him. She smiled and stepped in front of him, taking his old sword from him so as not to dull the edge of her own. Hubert joined her and the two took turns hacking at the same spot. The stones broke, but slowly.

Edmund eyed the faint flickering of the torch from where Liara had wedged it. It was starting to burn low. If they didn't get through soon, they would be left in complete darkness. Still, Liara and Hubert kept attacking the stone, the sounds of their struggle echoing down the hall.

Suddenly, the light got brighter. Edmund's eyes darted to the torch again. It had nearly sputtered out by this point, which meant…

"Stand aside," an unfamiliar voice commanded.

The three members of the City Watch spun around to see a Paladin standing in the passage, a fresh torch in his hand. Surprisingly, his sword remained in its sheath. Liara and Hubert stepped in front of Edmund, against his protests.

"Back away now, traitor. You face loyal members of the City Watch of Illux, and we fear no Paladins," Liara said. "You may join those slumbering here, or you may leave."

"You really think you could take me?" the Paladin asked.

Liara nodded at the corpses to either side of her. "All I see are dead Paladins around us. I like my chances."

The Paladin laughed. Something about his mirth was familiar to Edmund. The City Watchman searched the brown face of the Paladin for anything else that he recognized.

"I heard what you said to Arkon. The old bastard fumed about it for the rest of the day."

Then Edmund realized who he was, or at least who his family was.

"You are a Lighthammer," he said, pushing his way through his protectors.

"The same," the Paladin said. "Though that name means much less to me now than what it once did. I grew up in the shadow of my forebears, my father, and *my cousin.* I wanted to be like Devin ever since I was a boy. I was initiated with him and his friends.

"I had hoped that I would be able to fight alongside Devin, Trent, and the Seraph near the Great Chasm, but my father convinced Castille to keep me here. He wanted another Paladin in the family so that his line wasn't overshadowed by his sister's branch, but he didn't care if I became a hero. All he wanted were the titles and for me to sire more Lighthammers. Fuck the lot of them."

"Forgive me," Edmund said, his hands raised in a placating gesture. "I don't get along well with Lighthammers, as you mentioned. Your cousin though, he was a different sort. I hope that you are more like him than your father, but you must understand why I would be hesitant to trust you. How did you find us? If you're down here, you obviously serve Castille—so why wouldn't you kill us as soon as we put our guard down?"

The Paladin laughed again.

"I am no coward if that's what you are getting at. If I wanted the three of you dead, I could crush you into the same dust that surrounds you. I was down here helping Castille defile the graves of our ancestors for whatever nefarious purpose he claims the gods have set him to. When the fighting broke out, I decided to leave rather than kill those who would save the man who spit on my father. It was simple chance that I came this way, and then I heard your feeble attempts at cutting through the wall."

Not chance, providence.

The guards' torch sputtered out.

"Alright, Lighthammer," Edmund said.

"Arkos," the Paladin corrected.

"Of course." Edmund stepped aside and motioned for the others to do the same. "Please, be my guest."

The Paladin stepped forward and raised his right hand. Blue light filled the passage and the wall behind them exploded into a shower of debris.

As much as he had wanted to see the boy, Edmund had not dared to return to Elise's hovel. He was afraid to draw any attention to her. If Castille learned who she was, or who she had been hiding, he would surely put her and Ajax to death without a second thought. Instead, the three guards and the Paladin snuck their way out of the middle ring of the city where they had found themselves, and into the nearest safe-house that Liara could find.

She told Edmund that their people were scattered all over the city, waiting for the sign to show themselves again. What was left of the official City Watch was nothing more than a skeleton crew of those somehow more loyal to Castille than Edmund, or those too afraid to say otherwise. The majority had gone into hiding as soon as their captain had been taken.

So far, the lesser scion of the Lighthammer family had done nothing to arouse suspicion from the others. Indeed, Edmund saw more of Devin in him than he saw Arkon. Though he still refused to trust him completely, there was always the chance that Castille was using him to flush the rest of the resistence guards out of hiding.

Xyxax take him if he betrays us.

The family whose home they were staying in sat in the corner, eyeing the Paladin warily. They had learned over the last few days that the Paladins remaining in Illux were no longer protecting them in the same way that they had been before. It didn't matter that many good Paladins had returned to the city with Tess—all the people of the slums saw were inner city thugs crushing them under their heels.

"What's the plan?" Hubert asked as he drained a mug.

"Yes," said Merrin, a city watchman who had been hiding here already.

Edmund was busy dressing himself in spare armor that had been hidden here. It didn't fit him quite right, but it would have to do.

"It's simple, really," he said. "We can't do this alone. We need all of the allies that we can get, and we need to do something that will alert everyone in hiding that I am back."

"And don't forget that we don't trust Castille to keep the outer walls safe," Liara said, as if reading his mind.

Edmund smiled.

"Yes. The only way we take Illux is to take the walls back first. And we are starting with the gatehouse where those bastards betrayed us. I want to get the gates open in case any of Tess's people are still out there. A Demigod or two would change things. They aren't manning the outer wall with more than a token force. Once the wall is ours, word will spread, and the others will come out of hiding."

"What of Castille?" Arkos asked. "And the Divine Beast?"

"The Guardian was seen heading to battle beyond the wall. I doubt the Seraph would risk exposing himself like that. If he is smart, he won't let the enemy know that a new Seraph even resides in Illux until they have breached the city. No, I don't expect us to see Castille outside of the inner city anytime soon. Do you know why he was gathering the dead?"

"I do not. Even my father objected until Castille spoke to him in private. Then he told me to stop asking questions and help the Seraph with whatever he asked. All I know is that Castille claims that the Gods of Light have shown him a path to victory. Why that path requires the exhumation and defiling of our sacred dead I don't know."

"It's horse shit," Liara chimed in. "He's trying to unnerve those who would stand against him, that's all."

Edmund shot her a wry grin. She had always been capable before, but her confidence had grown tenfold since his incarceration. Having leadership thrust upon you certainly could do that to a person, he mused. After all, the same had happened to him.

"I hope you're right," Edmund sighed, "but I'm not so sure. A few hours ago, I would have said Castille ripping open the catacombs was horse shit, and yet here we are."

"And yet here we fucking are," Liara complained.

The mother of the house covered the ears of her children and scowled at them.

"Apologies, ma'am," Liara said.

"How many can you gather in the next few hours?" Edmund asked. "I want to strike before they realize that we made it out of the maze."

Liara smiled again. "We're in the slums, sir. Give me an hour and I can have a hundred."

It wasn't quite a hundred that walked with Edmund, but it felt like a thousand. The deserted members of the City Watch walked in a loose crowd, trying to look like a ragtag band of refugees and failing spectacularly. Edmund hoped that until they reached the wall, they wouldn't find any actual Paladins. Arkos told them that Castille had ordered everyone not actually manning the wall to stay within the inner city in case of a breach.

As they walked, real refugees and citizens of the slums slowly attached to them, arming themselves with cudgels and rusty blades. Edmund wasn't sure if they simply thought that his force was going to attack the inner city for more rations, or if they somehow knew who they were and what their cause was. It didn't matter, they bolstered the ranks; the Paladins were certainly no friends of theirs.

The midday sun was again moving earthward, leaving the side of Aenna, when the gates of the city rose above them. The gatehouse sat off to the side, a large structure made of the same white stone as the wall itself. It had multiple levels, reaching all of the way to the top of the wall, with small windows and murder-holes cut into it every few feet. These gatehouses were large enough to house a small fighting force and had often served as command centers for the City Watch. Edmund hoped that no more than a few Paladins would be stationed inside.

No sooner had the thought left his mind, than a horn blew from one of the upper levels. Arrows fired down from the gatehouse, cutting down several guards in the front row. The others threw off their cloaks and pulled free their weapons.

"We retake Illux today!" Edmund shouted. "For the people! For the High God!"

The City Watch and their band of refugees charged ahead, howling madly as more arrows and crossbow bolts rained down on them. The front door of the gatehouse was thrown open and half a dozen Paladins streamed out. Before they could react, Arkos Lighthammer removed all doubt of his allegiance as blue fire incinerated an unsuspecting Paladin.

"Traitor!" One of the others shouted, as shielding magic flared to life.

The City Watch slammed into the remaining Paladins in a savage wave of desperation. The Paladins didn't stand a chance. Edmund tried to keep himself back as best as he could. He was still weak from the last several days of imprisonment, even with the healing given to him by Arkos.

In front of him, a Paladin fought off ten refugees, snarling like the cornered animal that he was. Edmund wiped the sweat from his brow and forged ahead, waving a few others to follow him. The Paladin cut a man down just in front of Edmund, spraying the Captain of the City Watch with a gout of warm blood. Edmund ducked under the collapsing corpse, stabbing upward at the Paladin. His strike missed and he was sent careening into the sparring crowd. When he looked up, the Paladin was already falling under a dozen blows. Edmund noticed several arrows were buried in his neck.

The archers.

Edmund looked up and saw the windows filling with more guards. Their enemies were falling back, and if he didn't get to them soon, they would make quick work of the fighters on the ground. Edmund found Liara in the fray and pulled her behind him as another volley landed around them, killing and wounding several. They made it to the door of the gatehouse just as a lone guard was swinging it shut. Liara forced the door open, knocking the man backward. Edmund sprung in behind her, stabbing the man up through his chin. Crimson ran down Edmund's hand as he pulled the sword free. He pushed the traitorous guard away and bolted up the steps in the back of the sparsely furnished room.

On the next level, they found several dozen guards releasing arrow after arrow into the crowd below. Edmund rushed to the nearest window, tackling two of the unsuspecting archers out of the gatehouse. He twisted around just as a crossbow bolt punched into his shoulder. Liara slid beside him, cutting the arm off of the woman holding the crossbow. She screamed and stumbled back, sliding down the wall. Liara's sword flashed again and again, cutting down the rest of the archers before they had time to react.

"Are you alright?" She asked, wiping her blade on the cloak of one of the dead archers.

"I'm fine," Edmund grunted, pulling the bolt free. Thankfully, it had only stuck in the topmost layer of skin.

"A few more levels," Arkos said, appearing on the stairs. He had dozens of guards at his back.

Edmund nodded and led the way up the stairs. They made quick work of the archers on the other floors, ending all of the resistance in the gatehouse in a matter of minutes. When the killing was finished, the majority of the guards and refugees filtered back down to the street, clearing the dead from the road and setting up makeshift barricades in case Castille's loyalists came to retake the gatehouse.

Edmund, Liara, and Arkos traveled to the top of the gatehouse and stepped out on the wall. Outside of Illux, the two opposing armies of Demons and Accursed continued to do battle. From this distance, it was hard to tell the difference between the combatants. In the sky to the east, several Divine Beasts did battle. Edmund was sure that one of them looked like the Guardian of Illux.

The City Watch took control of the wall defense, manning the ballista that had been abandoned to protect the guardhouse. Edmund looked down past the gate for any sign of Tess and the Demigods. The area in front of the gate was blackened as if by fire, and naught was left but a few piles of bones. He sighed and turned to walk back to the gatehouse when an exasperated guard ran up from the lower levels.

"Sir! Sir! Captain! You must see this!" he panted.

Edmund and the others followed the man back down two levels. The floor of the room here was still slick with blood. Several guards were standing in front of a door that led to a storage closet. Edmund shouldered past them and audibly gasped.

A woman was bound on the floor of the closet. Her armor was covered in soot, as was most of her hair and body, but that didn't hide the distinctive white streak on her head.

A Demigod. Thank the High God.

Edmund quickly knelt and cut the woman free.

"What happened out there?" he asked. "How did you get back into the city?"

"I flew," she said, rubbing her wrists.

"Of course," Liara said, pushing her way up next to them. "It was either that or you tunneled."

"What of Tess and the others?" Edmund asked.

"I don't know," the woman said, her voice crestfallen. "We were attacked by a Divine Beast just as soon as we found the gate closed. We were able to fight the creature off, though it killed many of us. Tess sent me over the wall to see why the gate was shut. No sooner had I landed, than I was tied up and thrown in here. I take it you didn't see the rest of my kind still out there?"

"No, they aren't out there. Not near the gate, anyway. High God willing, they're holding out somewhere else. Arkos!" Edmund turned and waved the Paladin closer. "Do you have enough energy to help this woman?"

The Paladin nodded and placed glowing hands on her. Almost instantly, some of the color returned to her face.

"Can you fly back over the wall and look for them?"

The woman nodded.

"Tell Tess that the gate will open for her this time. We've had some troubles of our own inside the city, but this gate is ours again."

The Demigod stood and followed some of the other guards back up the steps. In moments, she was gone. Edmund sent the others below, leaving just him, Liara, and Arkos in the room.

"What's next?" Arkos asked.

"We have to hold this gate at all costs. I will not leave Tess and the Demigods out there to die. Gods help me, they will be the ones to pull us through all of this."

"Word will spread," Liara said. "Loyalists will flock to this gate, as will Castille's forces. We have to be ready for an assault. If we could take this gatehouse, so can they."

"We will be ready for them. Once we have more guards, I want us to take the rest of the wall, gate by gate. Then the slums. Let Castille hold the inner city. The cowards can rot there."

"EDMUND! EDMUND!"

He heard his name chanted by the crowd below. The three companions walked to the window and looked out. An even larger crowd of City Watch, refugees, and regular citizens had gathered on the street below. They continued to chant even louder when they saw Edmund looking out of the window.

"EDMUND! EDMUND!"

Liara cracked a smile. "Well, give 'em what they want."

"What is that?"

"You."

Edmund leaned back out the window and swallowed. He had given rousing speeches before, several times in the last few days in fact, but never to a crowd such as this. He closed his eyes for a moment and then pulled out his sword, raising it to the sky.

"Who's city is it?"

"OUR CITY!"

"Does the inner city rule here?"

"NO!"

"Can they take it from us?"

"NO!"

"If we work together, they cannot stand before us! We will take Illux back from this false Seraph and his bootlickers! We will hold Illux against all who come for it!"

"YES!"

"Whose city is it?"

"OURS!"

"Then stand with me and fight for it!"

The roar of the crowd was deafening. Edmund felt a supreme feeling of satisfaction swell up inside of him. He looked to Liara for approval. She was beaming. Beside her, Arkos nodded.

"EDMUND! EDMUND! EDMUND! EDMUND!"

9

Silver blood ran through his fingers. He ached all over, but the sharp pain in his abdomen bit at him again and again as if Luna was continuing to drive the blade deeper and deeper. Samson shuddered as his mind replayed the scene. His final companion had betrayed him. Just when he had dared to think that the stain of Lio was going to be washed from the Divine Plane, his entire world had spiraled.

He drained the goblet of liquid and let the cup fall from shaking fingers. The branches of Ayyslid caught the cup and absorbed it back into the wooden floor. There wasn't much left for Samson to do but wait for death. Gods had no Divine Spark, no soul to return to the High God. He was an empty shell of power, and that power was slowly draining out onto the floor.

Even the Seraph had abandoned him. And who could blame her? He had never given Ren anything more than his disdain, and now even regret seemed like too good a punishment for him. The Divine Beasts wouldn't speak to him either. All of them knew that he was going to die as an arrogant coward who was getting just what he deserved. Still, he wouldn't stop trying to do something to change the outcome of the war below. He owed them all that much, at least.

Guardian. Don't listen to her. She's with him now.

Silence.

Someone had awakened the Guardian of Illux, and Samson doubted that it was Ren. The last time they had spoken, she had yet to reach the City of Light. He imagined that, with Trent dead, she would be a fiery force of retribution when she reached Illux—if it wasn't already too late. So that meant that someone in the city awakened the Divine Beast. Unless Luna and Lio had discovered some mechanism for freeing those giant monstrosities that he was unaware of, Luna had given her blood to another.

Castille.

More regret washed over him. His previous respect for the old Paladin turned bitter in his mouth. Castille was a blunt instrument. He would never question the missives of his gods. That had made him an ideal candidate for becoming the next Seraph when the Pact still reigned and Luna still fought for the Light. Now, it meant that a zealot ruled Illux, dancing on the strings of a madwoman with no way to see the truth. This meant that when Ren did arrive at Illux, she would not meet the warm welcome that she was expecting.

Do I warn her? Or do I let her forge ahead to join her lover by the High God's side?

He thought of trying to make his way to the Basin and gaze out of Aenna to confirm his suspicions. Samson knew that this would be fatal. No matter what Ren called him, he would not throw the last of his life away. Not yet. There were still three living gods opposed to him outside of these walls. If he left Ayyslid, they would surely set upon him at once.

His wound continued to drain silver liquid. He would heal, in time, if he chose to. At this moment, he had yet to allow that to happen. His energy had been spent trying to listen to the prayers of those trapped in Illux, awaiting the end. For what it was worth, they made him feel less alone, if only slightly.

Guardian. I implore you to listen to me. The true Seraph comes to Illux. She is not your enemy. Luna and Lio work in concert.

Though the beast still refused to answer him, Samson could feel its mind for a fleeting moment. It seemed that the Guardian of Illux pitied him.

Wonderful.

Samson forced himself up out of his chair and walked to the wall behind it. An alcove opened, revealing dozens more goblets, each filled with his favored ambrosia. He grabbed two, draining one and throwing it over his shoulder. He touched the second one to his lips when he felt the entire fortress shudder. The glowing golden light of Ayyslid darkened, and the branches began to emerge from their tightly woven floors and walls, swinging madly. Someone was here, and the fortress was fighting them off.

The God of Light swore and drained the second cup, letting it fall to the ground. To his shock, it clattered onto the floor and rolled away. He reached his hand out and a branch quickly met him, wrapping around his arm. The branch went still and he broke it off from the wall, a wooden weapon now covering his dominant hand. Another branch wrapped his midsection, protecting the wound in his belly. The remaining branches stopped flailing and pointed to the eastern wall.

"Begone!" A female voice shouted.

The yell was followed by two booming cracks. The entire fortress began to shudder. Again the thunderous noise, and again Ayyslid shuddered. Samson nodded and the boughs at the far wall spread apart, just as the flails of Rhenaris passed through where they had been. The Goddess of Darkness nearly stumbled into the room.

Samson didn't pause.

He sprang at her, swinging his wood-covered arm at her head.

She wrapped it with one of the flails and yanked the branch clean off of him. Without slowing, he opened his hand and another branch filled it, this time shaped like a great hammer. Rhenaris swung both of her flails toward him, but Ayyslid caught her attack, wrapping her arms with dozens of lithe branches. Samson struck her in the face, cracking her neck. Her grey head and all of her spines went limp.

The God of Light raised his weapon again to finish her, but something bade him to stop. Rhenaris was fleeing from the Fallen One when he had seen her last. If she wasn't working with the two former Gods of Light, then why would she have come here? He dropped the hammer and it was absorbed back into the floor. With a flick of his wrist, the branches pulled her back to the wall as it closed behind her. Rhenaris's arms were pinned, and her head was held upright. Her eyes fluttered momentarily but never opened.

Samson walked back to the alcove and pulled out another goblet. He showed a surprising amount of self-control as he sipped on it while walking back toward his new guest. Once he reached her, he splashed the remaining ambrosia on her face. The goddess sputtered awake, glaring at Samson while the golden liquid ran down her body.

"Not the welcome I expected from the last God of Light," she hissed.

"I could get you a cup, if you'd like?" Samson mocked.

Rhenaris spat at him, and her spines all raised. Then her face softened somewhat.

"I came to offer you a truce," she whispered.

Samson laughed hard enough that it hurt the wound in his belly.

"Are you mad? Or did seeing Luna with the Fallen One simply make you jealous?"

"Neither. I'm sure you are too oafish to have noticed, but

Vardic and I had nearly killed the Fallen One before you intervened. This entire war would have ended if you hadn't—"

"I don't need your lies!" Samson cut her off. "I saw you fleeing like a scolded child before we even got to Infernaak. Vardic nearly killed him, it's true, but my intervention did nothing so far as prolonging this war. You would have simply taken control of the army outside of Illux for yourselves and finished what he had started. Do you not have your own army fighting there, even as we speak?"

Her eyes flashed. "That could change," she whispered.

"You're right. Your army could get defeated by his, and then he will overrun Illux. Even now, those two have taken the city from the inside by corrupting a new Seraph. I don't need your empty promises. And I certainly don't need an ally."

Rhenaris stared at the wood wrapped around his midsection like a girdle. She licked her lips and smiled widely.

"Looks would say otherwise, Samson. You very much need an ally. Your firewood of a fortress might have stopped me, but what of Luna and the Fallen One? Do you know if it would even try to stop them if they returned to their home? Would you even last that long? With Vardic dead, I have full control of the Demons, Accursed, and beasts that harry the flank of Lio's army. If you wish, I could order them to retreat. I would even be willing to have them escort your Seraph into the city."

Samson felt his golden face grow flush. He wasn't posturing as well as he had hoped.

"Together is the only way we stop this madness. Once it's done, we can go back to trying to kill each other, or we can even broker a peace. I care for nothing but survival at this point. And you are my only chance at that."

"I cannot deny that you speak the truth. When Ren makes it to Illux, she cannot win fighting on two fronts..."

Will she understand if I forge an alliance with one such as this?

The branches of Ayyslid started to slacken her bonds. As she got loose, Samson looked her over. He felt himself blushing again as he looked at her exposed mid-section.

High God help me.

Rhenaris dropped to the floor and slicked back the spines on her head.

"So, what'll it be, Samson? Survival?"

His mouth was dry. He ignored her and went back to the alcove, grabbing two goblets.

10

Ren flew just above Tyr. The Balance Monks and white tigress clung desperately to the feathers of his back, and if she tired before the Divine Beast did, she would most likely join them. Though they moved faster without the army behind them, they were still slower than Ren would have liked. It was the only way that Yyn could carry Aion; the golden ape hung from the dragon's claws like a doll.

Beside her, Lythe undulated through the air. The silver snake hissed in distaste every-so-often. Ren supposed that she would never be happy again, with her creators gone mad and one of her closest companions dead by Ren's hand just days before. Just as Lythe was the last of Ash Company, Ren felt like she was the last of her companions as well. Arran was dead nearly twenty years. Her parents were gone. Trent… Those she flew with were possibly the only friends she had left, and she had barely known them more than a few weeks. After winning this war, what would she have left? Would she still rule Illux?

Will they still want me?

Her hands brushed the hilt of Nightbreaker. The sword was a

covenant between her and the people of the Mortal Plane. So long as she carried it, she would fight for them. No matter how alone she was.

Below them was a sea of trees. Few forests south of the Rim were as large as this one. The army would have to go around, which would slow them by another day, she reckoned.

"What were they like?" Ren shouted over the wind whipping in her ears.

"Who?" Lythe hissed.

"Ash Company. Daniel. Springjack. All of them. The heroes of all of our stories."

And the villains.

The snake tasted the air with her tongue before replying.

"I didn't know Daniel and ssSpringjack asss well asss Asssh Company," Lythe replied. "SSSpringjack wasss quiet."

If she had been physically capable of laughing, Ren imagined that Lythe would have. The Seraph rolled her eyes.

"Merek wasss a good man. I don't know what happened to make him the way that he wasss when you met him. He had been brave onccce. He ssshamed me when I wasss not. Our firssst mission, we tracked a creature called Ar'Gorock the Cursssed. If not for him, we never would have killed it. That wasss the day we became Asssh Company."

Ren was familiar with the story. At least somewhat. The thought of learning about it from a being that lived it thrilled her. The trees vanished below them and the plains returned.

"He wasss a different kind of brave than Daniel," Lythe continued. "Daniel wasss the favored of Lio, but he alwaysss felt the need to prove himssself. Overcome hisss mark asss ssSinsssspawn. Merek didn't need to prove anything to anyone. He jussst did what he knew wasss right. That isss why he ssstayed loyal to Lio. Lio made him ssSeraph."

"I can't say I would have done anything differently," Ren mused, more to herself than the Divine Beast. "If the Gods of Light had asked me to wait my turn to die, or worse, sit by while my friends were butchered, I would have rebelled too. But Merek went beyond rebellion."

"Yesss," Lythe hissed, her voice sadder this time. "He fell to madnesss just as the othersss did it ssseamsss. He didn't ssserve the Light any longer. Maybe in the beginning he did what he thought wasss right. But by the end he wasss lossst."

"For what it's worth, I'm sorry I killed your friend."

"My friendsss all died when Ravim chained me beneath the earth. Now all that isss left is my duty. When thisss isss done, I can ressst again."

We all can.

The melancholy in the Divine Beast's voice almost made Ren regret asking about Ash Company. All of their remaining Divine Beasts had a sense of finality about them, as if they flew to their final doom, but Lythe seemed even more fatalistic than the others. Ren wasn't sure if they had truly done them any favors by freeing them.

"When we get through this, I want you to tell me about the others. Talking about them keeps them alive."

"Yesss," was all she said.

In the distance, Ren caught a glimpse of farmland, and behind it, the shadowy outline of a village. Even from here, she knew it instantly. This was the place where she had grown up. This was the place that she had saved from an attack by the Herald when she and Arran were both fresh Paladins. Ahead was Amel.

Ren leveled herself with Tyr and pointed to the village. The great owl nodded and the group adjusted their course. Lythe wasn't the only one who was going to reminisce about those they had lost, it seemed. Happiness and pain mingled in this place, and Ren wanted the opportunity to bask in both, one last time.

In a few moments, they landed in one of the tilled fields. Plows were left unmanned, and carts were overturned. A few goats wandered alone, eating whatever they could find. Ren felt her stomach tighten. Perhaps she shouldn't have come here. Seeing her home abandoned like this was too close to every fear she ever had growing up. Even though all of the people were safe in Illux, something about the shell of the village sickened her.

"Why did we come to Amel?" Teo asked as he hopped down from Tyr.

"I don't know," Ren admitted. "I guess I needed to say goodbye. I grew up here. My parents are buried here."

"Take all the time you need," Rella said. "The Divine Beasts could use the rest."

"Yes," Yyn thundered. "A thousand years of slumber haven't done Aion any favors."

The golden ape laughed. It was good to see the rest of them in good spirits. Ren nodded to them and walked into the village alone. Divinity started after her, but she waved the great cat off. She wanted to do this completely alone.

Once she reached the outskirts of the village, the empty buildings rose up to welcome her. Images flashed through her mind of the battle in the darkness here all those years ago. The enemy had attacked at night. Ren and Arran had been sent with a small force under the command of a Paladin called Kane. All because Arran had a vision of Amel getting attacked...

They came from the shadows in waves. The Paladins had set up a perimeter of torchlight around the city while the villagers, including Ren's parents, hid in the center of town. The Demons and Accursed nearly overwhelmed the defenders, until quick thinking by Ren rallied the villagers to come to their own defense. They held off the attacking forces and thwarted the Herald's plan. Arran and her parents had fought by her side that day.

You saved us.

Their words came to her again. So much of her life had

happened because of that night. If she hadn't saved Amel, she might not be Seraph now. Castille would very probably have taken Jerrok's place after his death. Gods be good, Jerrok himself might still be alive. After all, it was his confidence in Arran and her gift that fueled his crusade against the Forces of Darkness.

The homes were clustered closer together as Ren walked into the center of the village. She stopped at the well near the Paladin Lodge, lowering the bucket until she heard the familiar slosh of water. She raised it again and drank. It tasted just as she remembered: crisp and clean compared to the water in Illux. Her parents had been right to move out here. Ren sat the bucket down and looked around the square. A small chapel to the right caught her eye. Behind it, she knew she would find the graveyard where her parents were buried.

The Seraph opened the rotting wooden door and stepped into the chapel of the Gods of Light. She thought to bow her head in deference as she walked past the altar but changed her mind at the last second. Two of the Gods of Light had turned to Darkness, one was dead, and the last didn't deserve her respect. Their entire religion had fallen apart in a matter of days.

She opened the large door at the back of the sanctuary, which led up to the simple graveyard that had served Amel for generations. Each village buried their dead in different places. Some chose a place away from town, while others tried to replicate the catacombs of Illux. Amel had simply chosen to keep their dead close to their gods.

The spot in which Nirobe and Joran were buried was a corner plot, away from the tight cluster of the other graves. The people of Amel had given them special deference when each of them passed. Not only had they been pillars of the community, but they were the parents of the Seraph. Ren walked over to the two small markers and knelt. No sooner had her knees touched the ground, than the tears started. Grief really didn't get easier with time.

"I miss you both," she whispered. Then the words started to spill out. "I guess you know that. There is so much I want to tell you. I need you. I need your advice now more than I ever have before. But you can't give it to me. I have to do this alone, and I don't know if I can. I thought I was going to have Trent with me through this, but he was taken from me, just like you were. Hopefully, you three are at the High God's side together. Watch over him, will you? He isn't as smart as he thinks he is. I love you, mom. I love you, dad. I think I'll be seeing you soon."

Ren stood and turned back toward the chapel. She nearly jumped from her skin. Standing in the shadows of the doorway was a figure. Anger flashed over her. It seemed that one of her companions had ignored her desire to be alone with her parents. The figure didn't move when the Seraph started to stomp toward it. As she got closer, the figure faded back into the darkness of the chapel.

Now, she was concerned that they weren't alone here. Ren drew Nightbreaker and ran into the chapel. She saw no signs of the other visitor, but the front door was once again ajar. Looking back out to the square, Ren saw the figure moving down the street past the Paladin Lodge. What little she could make out was an older woman with dark hair and skin. Her heart skipped a beat. From the back, the woman almost looked like her mother.

"Wait!" she called out, sheathing Nightbreaker.

Who is that?

Ren ran out of the chapel and toward where she had last seen the woman. She rounded the corner just as the figure vanished down another street. The Seraph took to the air to catch up to the mysterious woman. As soon as she was airborne, she realized that somehow the woman had completely vanished. She wasn't walking where she should have been. Ren flew in circles for a few minutes before landing again.

"Hello!" She called out. "Who are you?"

"Come, sweet thing," a voice answered.

Ren spun around to face the source of the voice. She saw the woman standing in the doorway of her parent's old home. From here, there was no mistaking who this woman was. Somehow, it was her mother, and she was beckoning for Ren to join her inside the house.

Every logical part of her cried out in alarm. This must have been a hallucination or a trap of the gods. There was no way that Nirobe stood before her. The woman had been dead for years. Ren had buried her herself. Did her Divine Spark somehow return to the Mortal Plane?

"Mother?" Ren asked, her voice cracking.

Nirobe motioned again but said nothing. Then she turned and disappeared inside the house. This time Ren ran after her.

Ren burst through the door that her dead mother had been occupying just moments before. She found herself inside the main room of her childhood home. The new occupants hadn't changed much. The floor had the same divots and scuffs that she remembered. The smell of the wood and the thatched roof filled her with a sense of nostalgia. The Seraph scanned the room for any sign of her mother, but there was nothing.

That was when she saw it.

Ahead, lying propped against the side of the hearth was her mother's old walking stick. It was a long mahogany staff that had been carved by Ren's grandfather. The staff was covered in the faces of the Seraphs from Fiora to Jerrok. She had been fascinated with those faces as a child, and her parents had filled her head with the stories of those mighty beings.

Ren walked over and picked up the walking stick, running her fingers over the faces of her forebears as she had done so many times in her youth. Near the bottom, she noticed something that she had never seen before. Carved into the wood, just beside Jerrok, was her own likeness. The resemblance was uncanny—far better than the carving of Jerrok, compared to the real thing. Her grandfather had only carved the Seraphs based on what he thought they looked like, or in the case of Jerrok, from glimpses that he caught from afar. But this carving of her, this had been done by someone who had known her.

"Mother?" Ren said aloud. "Did you do this?"

The woman did not reappear, but Ren knew that it had to have been true. Nirobe had never told her that she was adding Ren to the staff that her grandfather had made. She didn't realize that the old guardwoman even had the skill to do so, and yet here she was: the last Seraph.

The last Seraph.

Ren clutched the staff against her body. She knew what it was that she needed to do. She knew why she needed to find this. If she survived the siege of Illux, she would no longer rule the people of the Mortal Plane. She would leave them to make their own fate and join the other faces on the staff as a piece of history.

The last Seraph stood and carried her mother's walking stick with her as she returned to her companions. Soon, they would reach Illux. Soon, they would reach war.

11

The dark smudge on the horizon was undoubtedly Ren's army. The people of Seatown marched toward Illux, just as she had hoped. Trent wondered if they would have followed him if he had been the one Seraph left to guide them. He wasn't half the leader that she was. Thank the gods the world had her. Thank the gods that he did.

"What's that?" his father shouted. "My eyes aren't what they used to be."

"Looks like Ren's army."

He still wasn't comfortable talking to his father. He still wasn't comfortable calling the man *father*. He doubted that he ever would. With any luck, one of the two of them wouldn't make it through the coming days, and he wouldn't have to live with the discomfort.

I can't think that way. He wants to make amends.

Trent's arms ached. Even with Divine Blood, he was exhausted from carrying the burden over the countless miles. A few weeks ago, if he had been in this position he would have dropped the man to his death. He nearly made that mistake back in Illux. If not for Devin he would have committed an unforgivable sin. If not for

Devin, he himself would be dead now. Devin had saved his soul, and he would not take that lightly. If not for himself, if not for Terric, Trent would at least forgive his father for Devin.

The wind changed, bringing with it the stinging smell of the army. It was the smell of sweat, fear, and shit. Trent wrinkled his nose in disgust. It reminded him of the slums. He certainly didn't miss that smell. When this was all over, if any of Illux still stood, Trent would find a way to rebuild the outer city of Illux. There would never be another man like his father made from the conditions of that city.

The Seraph started his descent, his arms aching more incessantly now that relief was so close. He flew over the top of the ragtag army, taking a mental note of its size. They were several thousand strong but considering their complete lack of training, it wasn't even close to enough. Once the people below saw the winged shape cutting over them, shouts began to rise up from the marchers. A loose arrow came short and fell back earthward. The army came to a halt just as Trent neared the front of the column.

Where are the Divine Beasts?

Trent landed, releasing his burden and stretching his shoulders as much as his armor allowed. In front of him, both Gil and the green-cloaked Seatown woman sat on horseback. The woman's face was an impenetrable wall. Gil's mouth hung wide open like he was looking at a ghost.

"Well," Trent said. "You aren't the only one who's hard to kill around here."

Gil jumped down from his horse and wrapped Trent in a tight hug. The Paladin wept openly. Trent could feel the crude sword that was grafted to Gil's arm press against his back. Even as he thought of it, the scars on his face tightened. Dodging death never came without a toll.

"Gods be good! You were gone—the Balance Monks saw you eaten by that Divine Beast!"

"I was. But somehow I blasted my way out and my father dragged me to safety."

"Your father?" Gil said incredulously.

By now, the first riders and marchers of the army had begun to form a half-circle around the Seraph and Paladin. Concerned whispers rippled through the crowd.

"Yes," Trent said, nodding at the man called Brandon. "A gift from the High God no doubt, but a story for another day. Where is Ren?"

Gil's eyes fell for a moment.

"It seems your reunion was not yet meant to be. She and the Balance Monks have gone ahead with the Divine Beasts. The gods told her that the defense of the city was going poorly. Ren decided to do what they could to turn the tide before we arrived."

Without another word, Trent motioned for his father. They would return to the sky and try to catch up to Ren. He would not lose her. He nodded to Gil and started to spread his wings when the woman in green finally spoke.

"Wait, Seraph!"

Trent stopped, folding his wings. His arms thanked her for the continued respite.

"I know you wish to help the Lady Ren, but I implore you, stay with us," she said. "My people march to save a city that never gave a damn about them. Most of them still think that they are never going to see their own loved ones again. They think they will die saving those who would not have saved them. Ren did what she thought was best for Illux, but I need someone to do what is best for these people. We need a Seraph to fight with us."

Though her plea was heartfelt, Trent wasn't going to allow anyone to stop him from returning to the woman he loved. She was flying right into the jaws of the beast, and he wasn't there to help.

"I appreciate your words, but I have been parted from her for too long," Trent said.

"Listen to her, Trent," Gil said. "If not for these people, then for me. Ren can take care of herself more than you ever could. You know that. Seraph or not, you are still a lovestruck little boy at heart. If she is in danger, the last thing she needs is you mucking things up. The people of Seatown are still our people. You marching with them would make them feel safer. It would show them that we are all in this together."

"But—" Trent began.

"Son," his father cut him off. "I have no right to tell you what to do ever again. But your friend is right. I lived in Seatown for the last several weeks. These people need a sign that Illux has not forsaken them. They need to know that the gods haven't forsaken them. They need *you*."

Trent felt the tension begin to leave his body. He was so close to being reunited with her. So close.

"I need you," Gil said, his body wracked by quiet sobs. The Paladin hugged Trent again. "I've lost my way, Trent. None of it makes sense anymore. Without Devin, without you, I—I…thought I knew the right thing to do, but I don't. I need to save these people. Not just Illux, but the people of Seatown too. I can't do it alone."

Trent held his friend close, even as he noticed the crowd watching them was growing larger by the moment. His eyes met that of the woman and he nodded. She motioned and two horses were brought forward for Trent and his father.

"I will march with you," Trent shouted to the crowd as he let go of Gil. "This fight is for all of the Mortal Plane, so we must all fight together. You do not know me, but you can see that I am indeed another Seraph. The Goddess Arra chose me as she lay dying to carry out her will. She would not have forsaken you, and neither will I."

A rumble of approval moved through the crowd. Trent and his father got onto their new horses and the march resumed.

I hope I'm doing the right thing.

The woman in green road beside him. She leaned close enough that no one else could hear her.

"My name is Wyn Thacker," she said. "I am the Admiral of Seatown, as was my father before me. He saw the damage that the Paladins of Illux could pose to the rest of us. Our city burned from the madness of Cecilia Whitethorn. Then to my shame, I allowed the Ten to hang my people in the square. Make no mistake, I have no love for the will of the gods or the bearers of Divine Blood. But I am a woman of honor, and I have my own sins to atone for. We march because Ren promised us that we could be free from the yolk of Illux. I expect you to honor that arrangement if she cannot."

The implication of her last words hung in the air between them, making Trent regret his decision to leave Ren alone for the moment. He pushed the notion from his mind.

"I will," he said. "I've yet to rule over anyone. I grew up in the slums. I know what it's like to be on the bottom. It's past time for the order of things to be changed."

"Good," she said, smiling. "I'll leave you to your friend, then. He needs you more than I."

Wyn fell back to a group of riders just behind them. Her eyes never left Trent. Something about her manner made Trent uncomfortable. He could tell that she would do anything for her people—even slit his throat if needed.

Trent guided his horse closer to Gil. His father rode off to the side, giving them space. Honestly, Brandon just looked happy to be riding on a horse rather than dangling in the sky.

"How did he die?" Gil asked.

Trent swallowed, hard. He had hoped that someone else would have told him by now.

"I—he—"

"I was told that he fought a Divine Beast singlehandedly."

"He did," Trent said softly.

"Where were you?" Gil asked, his tone less accusatory than his words.

"I was next to him. And then he..." Trent trailed off. After enough time passed that he figured that they should be at Illux already, he started again. "We tracked the enemy for weeks after we left Marna. Devin and I discovered that they were gathering near the Great Chasm. A band of Demons and Accursed ambushed us, and we nearly fell then. By some miracle, we made it back to Illux just as word of Marna's burning arrived. We both thought you had died. Devin was inconsolable. He would have killed Xyxax himself if the bastard had been standing there, and then drank a whole cellar's worth of wine afterward."

Gil cracked a slight smile.

"Ren put us in charge of the army. I love her, but that was probably a mistake. In any case, we marched from Illux and met them in the field, not far from where Devin and I found them. We did well at first, but there was no sign of the Herald. Devin fought like I had never seen before. He was truly the greatest member of his house in that battle. His uncle would have shit. But then..." Trent started to trail off again. His attempts at humor weren't helping like he had hoped. "The Herald and Akklor the Unbidden showed up. They tore through us. Hundreds died. The entire battle turned. The line broke. It seemed like it was all over. Devin and I tried to stop the bastard, but he was too powerful.

"We...tried to face it down together, knowing that we would die. But Devin, he...he pushed me out of the way and told me to look for him by the High God's side another day. I think he wanted to see you again. I'm sorry. I'm so sorry."

"What happened next?" Was all Gil asked.

"Devin jumped through the air and the thing caught him in its hand. He threw Broderick's axe and blinded that wretch before it crushed him. He died just like the heroes of old."

"I never doubted that. What of Akklor? The others told me it didn't survive the battle."

"It did not. I...I saw to that."

"Thank you, Trent," Gil said. "You know, sometimes I was jealous of you. Still, I know that he didn't love you the same way that he loved me. Even if you preferred men, he wouldn't have been interested. Too pale." Trent and Gil both chuckled. "But still, as a friend, he loved you like a brother. I often worried that he would choose you if forced. And then I decided to stay in Rinwaithe, and he did choose you. He would have rather been parted from me, than his brother."

Trent stayed silent. Gil's words brought more guilt welling up.

"It took me a long time to get over that one. A long time. Gods be good, I wished for you to break your neck more than once. But then I realized that what Devin and I had wasn't going to fade. I realized that I loved him because he was loyal and loved you so much. He was larger than life. He was one of the heroes of the old stories, and we were just side characters. Well, I was. You will get your own tales. But not me. I thought I was alright with that when you passed through Marna. I thought I was over it. He told me that night that he would love me until the day he died. He even promised that one day he would move out to the villages with me, if for no other reason than to get away from his family. And then you both died in battle, and I was left alone. I couldn't even die saving Marna. And I lost my way in Seatown, Trent. I shamed you both."

"You did nothing of the sort," Trent whispered. "I don't know what happened in Seatown, but I know you. You sell yourself short. You have always done the right thing for the people of this world. Whatever you did, you thought it was the right thing."

"Ask them that," Gil said, nodding at the people behind them.

"I don't need to," Trent said.

"I don't want to survive the battle, Trent," Gil said. "I want to see him again. That's all I want."

"You aren't giving up that easily. He would kick your ass if he were here. He kept me alive for a reason. Maybe it was so I could do the same for you."

"Maybe."

"We are all staring down our death," Trent said. "And it's in this moment that we get to be our best selves. May we all face the end as Devin did. Let them put *that* in the songs and stories."

12

The word from the outposts on the other side of Illux was that the second army of the enemy was finally pulling back. What that meant, beyond the obvious fact that the siege was going to get a lot more aggressive, was anyone's guess. The runner who had brought the news was an urchin boy who couldn't have been much older than ten. It was easier to use children to ferry messages between the various guard holdouts than to risk drawing the attention of the Paladin loyalists.

Open war had been declared between the inner city and the slums. Most of Illux belonged to Edmund now, due in no small part to the shortage of food and the general resentment toward Castille and his ilk. Still, the City Watch did not move openly except on the outermost edges of the city and along the wall. Not everyone in the slums was a friend.

"Thank you, boy," Edmund said. "Return to Hubert and make sure that he tells the others to be on alert. The hammer will fall anytime now."

The boy nodded and ran off, back down the alley behind them. Edmund was crouched behind an abandoned stall in one of the mid-city markets. This place had been empty since the riot that had killed Edmund's predecessor, Redrick. Beside him, Liara and Arkos hunkered down as well. They were watching with disgust as several City Watch members were hung over the makeshift wall that Castille had constructed.

Edmund recognized most of the bloated faces. They had been the very guards who had followed Liara and freed him from Castille in the catacombs. Those who weren't killed in the fighting down there had been captured and executed. One of Liara's spies had warned them that the fighters were to be hung from spots along the wall as a message.

The Captain of the City Watch clenched his fists. Castille and Yan would pay for this. Arkon Lighthammer would pay for this. He would burn the inner city if he had to. They had all abandoned their sacred oath to protect the people of this city. There was hardly a worse crime in his eyes.

Behind him, Edmund could feel Liara start to stand. He placed a hand on her to keep her crouched. Her anger was palpable. She most likely felt even more responsible than Edmund did for these deaths. She had been the one who had taken volunteers into the catacombs. It had been her mission and her people that were now being defiled.

They will pay. I promise.

"Now isn't the right time," he whispered. "We are trying to sneak into the inner city, remember? Not draw attention to ourselves. We won't leave them up there, I promise."

"This is too far, Edmund," she said through gritted teeth. "You and Arkos go in another way, they won't think to check the other walls if they are cleaning the blood off of this one."

"No," Edmund said. "That's an order."

Their spy had also told them that whatever purpose Castille had exhumed all of the dead from the catacombs for was taking place today, in front of the Grand Cathedral. While Liara had advised that they simply find out what had happened from her spies, Edmund had decided that he wanted to see for himself. He was tired of others putting themselves at risk for him. That wasn't why he was captain.

Edmund turned to sneak back down the alley so they could look for another way over when he saw Arkos standing. The Lighthammer Paladin smirked at Liara with that familiar, cocky smile of his.

"I'll get them down for you."

"I just said—" Edmund began.

"I am following you," Arkos retorted, "but I don't take orders from you. Sorry, Captain, but this is Paladin business."

Edmund felt his face grow red as he tried to open his mouth again but the Paladin walked past him. Liara grabbed his arm and pulled him back into the shadows of the market where they could see better.

"He's an asshole," she said, "but I like him."

"Of course you fucking do," Edmund muttered.

Arkos walked up to the wall with confidence and swagger that only an upbringing in the inner city could have afforded him. His sword remained in its sheath, and he had his hands raised in a placating gesture. The men hanging the corpses weren't Paladins as far as Edmund could tell. That alone was fortunate. As Arkos got closer, his hands dropped to his sides.

"Hello!" He shouted. "What in the High God's name are you doing?"

"None of your business!" Shouted one.

"Who's asking?" Asked the other.

They didn't seem too bright to Edmund. They certainly weren't favored sons of some old house. No doubt they were simply men who had chosen Castille because he claimed to be in charge, not because their families were sworn to him.

"I'm a Paladin. My name is Arkos Lighthammer. No doubt you know my family."

One looked at the other and then nodded.

"Good," Arkos continued. "Then I ask you again, as a Paladin of the inner city, what are you doing with those bodies?"

"By order of Castille, Seraph of this city," the left man began, clearly repeating a rehearsed line, "we are to hang these traitors as a message to all others. Now would you be so kind as to help us or bugger off?"

"I can't help you from down here. Open up and I'll do a bit of hanging."

The men looked at one another for a moment. The man on the right shrugged and disappeared down the steps on the backside of the wall. In a few moments, the door cut into the barricade swung open. Arkos walked through the opening, which quickly shut behind him. The next few moments dragged on while Edmund and Liara held their breath. Then, the Paladin was atop the wall, showing the men the proper way to prepare a noose.

Suddenly, Arkos kicked the legs out from under the man on the left, sending him sprawling. The Paladin slipped the noose over the man on the right and dropped him from the wall. His neck only partially snapped, leaving him flopping about beside the two bloated bodies that he had already hung. Arkos quickly pulled the corpses of the City Watchmen up and removed the ropes from their necks. Before the other man could stand, he was hanging beside his accomplice, his own movements even more frantic as he lost air.

The door to the wall flew back open, and Arkos walked out, carrying three men over his shoulders. He walked right past an incredulous Edmund and Liara before hiding the bodies in the stall.

"We will have to come back for them tonight. Then we can give them a proper burial, now let's go."

Edmund nodded dumbly.

As they walked to the wall, Edmund leaned in to Liara and whispered in her ear.

"I thought I was in charge, but after that...who would follow me over him?"

"You are in charge, sir," she said slyly. "Every good leader needs a flashy champion to do their dirty work."

"And if he decided that he wants to run the Watch instead of being my *champion*?"

"Well, I'd kill him. After sleeping with him, of course."

Arkos whistled as they walked underneath the twitching feet of the hanged men.

THE INNER CITY had less activity than they had expected. Either the families here were finally hiding out of fear, or they had all been conscripted into Castille's army. Edmund sighed. Even the stuck-up bastards of the inner city were still people that should be under his care. He tried to push that thought out of his mind. Their oppression needed to end. That was the only way the city would survive.

They came across a family or two clothed in clean silks who paid them no mind. Arkos looked the part of an inner city Paladin, and if any recognized him, they surely saw no reason to question a scion of the Lighthammers. Edmund and Liara were dressed finely enough that they didn't draw second glances, at least not while they walked with Arkos. If they ran into anyone who recognized them though, it would all be over.

As they got closer to the plaza of the Grand Cathedral, they began to keep to the shadows and alleys, staying away from the well-lit main thoroughfares. The number of people on the streets grew as they got closer to their final destination. It wouldn't be long before someone recognized them. Edmund needed to come up with something...

"Arkos?" a woman asked.

Edmund and Liara each dropped their hands to their weapons. The party turned around to see who was speaking. A young woman near Edmund's age waved in greeting. She was stocky and similar in general look to Arkos, so much so that Edmund thought she must have been another Lighthammer.

"Cousin," he said warmly. "I didn't expect to see you..."

"I mean, everyone was invited. What would your father think if one of the Lighthammers, even his cousin's daughter, didn't show up to Castille's big gathering?"

"What indeed?" Liara said wryly.

Edmund shot her a dark look.

Does anyone care what I think anymore?

"You probably know more than most," the girl said, whispering. "What is it that the old man has planned? They say he has come up with a weapon that can protect the city from any threat. That it will change the war. That it will retake the slums. Is that true?"

"You'll have to forgive me, cousin. I'm afraid I don't know any more than you. Father hasn't been sharing much with me," he leaned in with mock secrecy, "and to be honest, Castille has been sharing less with him than he used to."

"The scandal," she said. "And who is this with you?"

"Umm..."

"Trent and Elise," Edmund said quickly. "We are—were, members of the City Watch. Once that coward Edmund went rogue and betrayed Castille, we broke rank and swore our loyalty to—"

"Oh! It sounds like it's starting. See you, cousin!"

The woman turned and joined the crowd that had begun to press into the plaza. Edmund motioned for the other two to follow him. They slid out of the alley into the throng and tried to hide among the sea of people. The crowd filled the plaza, pressing tightly in a large circle around the Grand Cathedral. In the distance, Edmund could make out the crater where the Guardian of Illux had burst from the catacombs.

The three companions carefully pushed their way toward the front line of onlookers. This was when Edmund began to get nervous. The chances that they met another person who recognized them were high. Their only hope was that they would blend in with the mass of faces.

This was a mistake. I should have left it up to the spy.

Then Edmund saw what Castille had summoned them all for, and his misgivings were replaced with raw curiosity. Castille, Yan, Arkon, and a few others were standing on a makeshift dais so that they could be more easily seen. Spread out on the ground were hundreds and hundreds of armored corpses from the catacombs. Each of the bodies sat in depressions that had been carved into the cobblestone. Connecting the depressions were channels likewise cut in the ground.

"What in the High God's name is he doing?" Liara whispered.

"Blasphemy," Arkos said.

It seemed that Arkos wasn't alone in that sentiment, based on the general tone of the murmurs. Once the crowd finished filtering in, Arkon called the crowd to order. Even over the cacophony of the gathered multitude, Edmund could see that the sound of his father's voice made Arkos uneasy. Once they quieted down, Castille spoke.

"People of Illux!" He thundered. "I have gathered you here because the goddess has shown me the path to our salvation! She has given us the means to create an army that will never be defeated! I know you think we have dishonored our ancestors by removing them from the catacombs, but I swear to you that Luna herself has ordered it so! Begin!"

Castille waved and several Paladins standing next to giant

crucibles began heating their undersides with blue fire. Once the iron containers were glowing red-hot, they tipped them over, filling the channels with molten steel. The steel slowly ran down the channels and filled the depressions, covering the bodies of the dead Paladins.

"Luna, Goddess of Light, it is ready for you! Bless your faithful!"

Then the sky cracked with a peal of thunder. Aenna seemed to flash with a blinding light, and then a figure was floating gracefully down to the plaza. People began to cry out. Even Edmund was suddenly overwhelmed with reverence.

It can't be. It's not possible.

"Luna!" A voice cried.

"Goddess! Save us."

All around them, people began to wail and fall to their knees. One of the Gods of Light was again on the Mortal Plane. Edmund remembered what Tess had said Arra had been like. He felt Liara pull him to his knees. His eyes weren't on the goddess anymore but on her champion. Castille was standing at the edge of the molten steel, his face glowing from the heat. His expression was pure rapture.

When she was just above the plaza, the golden-skinned goddess outstretched her arms and pointed them at the bodies. Lightning arced from her arms, striking the molten steel in a thousand places. The very air hummed with the energy pouring off of the goddess. Heat bathed the kneeling crowd. Edmund felt the sweat forming on his brow, but he couldn't look away. For a fleeting moment, he was glad that he had not relied on the spy. He never would have believed it if he hadn't seen it with his own eyes.

The first silver arm reached out of the glowing molten rivulets. Then another. And another. Behind each arm, a hulking armored figure pulled themselves free of the glowing sludge and onto the cobblestones.

When they stopped glowing as they cooled, Edmund was able to make them out. They stood as tall as a Paladin, though somehow, they seemed even larger. All of them retained the armor that they had worn in life, though their mail was more reflective than it ever had been before, like polished glass. Most striking of all though, was the silver-skeletal head atop each set of soldiers. The eyes were hollow and empty like the helm of a Demon, but Edmund somehow knew that they could see just as well as he could.

Once all of the steel warriors had risen, the goddess stopped her lightning barrage. She hung over the newly created army for a few moments as if she were surveying her handiwork. She nodded to Castille and then addressed the gathered crowd as well as the metallic corpses.

"Behold my creation for you," her lyrical voice thundered. "These steel Paladins shall serve the Seraph of Illux. They draw their strength from me. They shall not age, nor feel fear or pain. They will serve as my instrument to wipe clean the sins of this world. I call them Tempest Born, for they were created during the storm of war."

"Luna!" The crowd cried. "Goddess of Light. You bless us!"

Edmund felt his stomach twist into knots. He tried not to wretch. One of the actual Gods of Light was on the Mortal Plane and she had just created an army of mindless golems to wage war on the slums. What could they possibly do?

While he was lost in thought, Luna returned to Aenna and vanished. The crowd continued to weep, even as Castille barked orders and the Tempest Born marched in line to the edges of the plaza. After a time, the crowd dispersed, and Edmund, Liara, and Arkos snuck out with them.

. . .

LATER THAT EVENING, the trio sat in the gatehouse they had taken days before. Edmund had doubled guard when they returned, but he doubted that it would help. He doubted that anything could stop the steel tide that was coming for them. Without some kind of miracle, they were going to be slaughtered within a fortnight. He considered telling everyone to stand down and turning himself back into Castille. What other option did he have?

We can fight. If we kill the Seraph, we kill the Tempest Born.

Arkos and Liara sat apart from him, talking as if nothing had changed. She told him bawdy tales and he laughed in great bellows that nearly shook the stones of the tower. Already, a plan was forming in his mind. They needed to get close to the Seraph again. He figured that Castille was arrogant enough that he would treat with Edmund if requested. It wouldn't be the most honorable way to kill an enemy, but…

"Captain! Captain!" a man shouted, bursting throw the door.

Edmund shot to his feet. His heart sank. He was too late. The Tempest Born were outside.

"What is it?" He asked.

"The Demigods have returned. They are at the gate."

Without another word, Edmund sprinted from the room. He took the stairs two at a time, his mind racing. This changed everything. Was Tess alive? With the Demigods, they stood a chance against the Tempest Born. They had a chance to kill Castille.

On the ground level, Edmund began shouting. "Open the gate! Open the gate!"

He ran out onto the street just as the gates began to grind open. He stood in the middle of the road, his breath caught in his throat. Liara and Arkos joined him moments later. Demigods poured through before the gate was finished opening. Many of them were gravely injured, with those faring better dragging their comrades inside. Edmund waved for his guards to help them inside. He searched from face to face for some sign of Tess.

Then he saw her.

She was bringing up the rear, carrying a young man with dark hair in her arms. She looked tired and dirty, but she was alive. When she got closer, she handed the man off to one of Edmund's people and walked up to the captain. He extended his hand. Instead, she struck him across the face.

"I'm tired of the damned gate closing," she said, taking him in her arms.

"I'm sorry," Edmund said weakly. "We, uh, haven't had the best of luck in here."

No sooner had the words left his mouth, than a section of the wall collapsed farther down the street. A Divine Beast pulled itself up from the rubble and shook the silt off. It was a giant hulking creature with several thick horns upon its snout. Edmund looked up to see that the ballista had been unmanned momentarily while the Demigods were entering the city.

The Guardian of Illux landed between the creature and the gatehouse, howling with rage.

The wall had been breached.

13

Illux appeared on the horizon. It was a shimmering beacon in a sea of darkness. Even from this height, Ren could see the swaths of Demons and Accursed pressing up against the walls like a dark tide. Her heart quickened as she thought of how badly this could be going already. It was a doomed effort. She was flying to her death. The Seraph gripped Tyr as she watched the city grow in size.

Beside her, the Balance Monks and Divinity clung for dear life. They still weren't as comfortable flying as Ren was. She did have a twenty-year head start on them, after all. Even behind the looks of mild panic and unease, she could still see the steely determination that both monks refused to give up.

If anyone can do this, it's us.

Still, she scanned the skies for other flying Divine Beasts. If they were attacked in the air, before they made it to Illux, Tyr would be hard-pressed to keep his charges from falling to their deaths. So far, it looked as if the skies were clear at this distance. Closer to the city though, Ren saw dark shapes in the air, flitting back and forth like carrion birds over the battlefield. What had stopped them from flying over the walls and making quick work of the defenders she wasn't sure.

Ren.

It was Samson again. She nearly rolled her eyes. Gods had the worst timing, it seemed. No matter, she would ignore him all the same. He wasn't her god anymore.

Ren, please listen. The wall has just been breached.

Ren nearly started. He wasn't going to the Basin. How could he know that specifically?

How do you know? Have you finally left Ayyslid?

No. But we are not without eyes down there anymore.

What are you talking about? Whose eyes?

You won't like this, but I need you to listen.

Ren looked up at Aenna. The pale disc hung beside the midday sun.

I'm listening.

Rhenaris and I have formed an alliance.

"What?" Ren said aloud. Her companions looked at her askance.

Luna and Lio are her enemies too. Listen—

You're a fool.

I'm a pragmatist. Now listen. Rhenaris and Vardic made their own Heralds and army. This army has been attacking the Fallen One's army at the flank. If not for this, Illux would have fallen days ago. After the death of Vardic, his Herald vanished, leaving Rhenaris in complete control. Her forces grow depleted, but they are going to mount one final attack to give you a chance to get into the city.

This is madness.

This is the only way. I need you to trust me. Lio's forces just breached the wall. There isn't much time.

You regret giving me your blood, now. See what happens if you betray me.

Samson remained silent.

"Apparently the last of the gods have gone mad," Ren shouted over the wind. "Rhenaris will be providing us an escort into the city. Lio has breached the walls. We will need all of the help we can get."

Rella and Teo looked at each other and nodded. They weren't strangers to alliances between previously at-war gods. Ren chuckled to herself. Did she fight for the Light any longer? Or was she an agent of Balance now?

The Divine Beasts don't believe me either. But they did say that they would do whatever you command.

Ren didn't answer him, but she did smile.

A winged shape appeared before them, small and humanoid. Ren prepared herself for a battle, but the Herald stopped short. This Herald was clearly female, with sickly pale skin and black veins that traced her body.

"I was told you were bringing an army? No matter, my forces will pull back after this," she barked. "We will keep them distracted so that you may get inside."

Ren nodded. The Herald spat and then winged her way back down toward the ground. Demons and Accursed swarmed to the Herald like insects to their queen as she approached the battlefield. Ren could see that they were clearing a path to the nearest gate. With any luck, they would be able to hold that position long enough for Gil and the army to make it to the city. Ren and the Divine Beasts had no need of a gate.

Her group flew toward the city with renewed haste. They couldn't risk drawing the attention of one of the Divine Beasts. Thankfully, all of the creatures seemed to be engaged with their counterparts from the other army at the moment.

A massive shape flew toward them, seemingly from inside the city. It was a Divine Beast whose shape Ren recognized from the tapestries inside the Fourth Spire. The Guardian of Illux. A wave of relief washed over her. Somehow, Illux had found a way to free a living weapon of their own.

How could they do that without Divine Blood?

Ren!

Without warning, the Guardian slammed into Tyr, sending the great owl careening through the air. Ren and the others fell from their mount as the world spun around them. In a moment of panic, Ren realized that she wouldn't be able to catch them all. The closest to her was Rella. Ren grabbed the falling monk under her arms. Teo and Divinity would stand no chance.

Then Tyr returned, silver blood staining his feathers. He swooped under the other monk and white tigress in a motion more dexterous than a creature of his size should have been able to. Ren let out a sigh of relief and angled herself for the far side of the wall. They didn't have time to return straight to the Fourth Spire, she would need to check on the defenses of the slums first.

The breach in the wall was close, with hundreds of dark shapes milling about the opening. Rhenaris's force was engaging the flanks of the invaders, keeping them from fully committing to the breach. The corpse of a large Divine Beast lay in the opening, further obstructing it. It seemed that the wall would still hold for a few short moments.

Ren landed in the street, returned at last to her city. Even amongst the chaos, she felt a wave of relief. If only Trent had been there with her…

Tyr and the other Divine Beasts landed beside her, shaking the ground and demolishing some hopefully empty homes. Once Teo and Divinity were on the ground, Tyr and the other flying Divine Beasts returned to the air.

"The Guardian has gone mad!" Tyr thundered. "He is a creature of Luna now! We must draw him away, lest he hampers our defense. With your leave, Lady Ren?"

"Do as you must, but try not to kill him!" Ren shouted. "We

need all of the help we can get. The rest of you, into the breach! Don't give them an inch of our city. It was for this reason you were made, and for this reason you were awakened! Protect Illux!"

Ren turned from the Divine Beasts to see a group of City Watch and soldiers running to her position. The soldiers looked haggard and battle-worn. She was certain that she recognized some of their faces from the battle near the Great Chasm. Strangely, each of them bore a bit of white hair along with their natural colors.

"The Lady has returned!" the front watchman shouted as he dropped to one knee. She recognized him as Edmund, one of the ranking members of the City Watch.

The others all followed suit, though Ren noticed a clear reticence from the soldiers. Something had changed.

"Tess?" Ren asked. The soldier closest to Edmund had been one of her commanders from the battle. Some *had* returned!

"My lady," Tess said, standing. "We saw you killed!"

"They haven't been able to manage that yet."

"Then Castille…" Edmund trailed off.

Ren thought to question his response when a contingent of Demons sprang into the street from the rent in the wall. Members of the Watch and the white-haired soldiers jumped into action, none waiting for Ren to command them. Gouts of red flame burst to life and were immediately beaten back by blasts of ice and walls of stone. Dozens of swords flew through the air as if they were a volley of arrows.

What in the High God's name?

The Seraph tried to ignore her confusion and join her troops against the enemy. It seemed that the Light had more tricks than just Ren and the Divine Beasts. Ahead, a Demon sprang into the air in an attempt to engage several members of the Watch at once. Ren slammed into the creature with such force that it broke against the wall of Illux behind it. Twisting, the winged warrior lanced lightning down the blade of Nightbreaker into another Demon. It crumpled into a smoldering husk.

Two more Demons approached her with a net and spears. How could they have known she was coming?

Luna. I will find a way to make you pay for this.

Don't count on it, dear.

Ren took to the air, just as the net landed where she had been standing. She smiled and swung about, preparing to end the threat once and for all. Without warning, Ren fell back to the ground, pain blossoming from her left wing. One of the spears had found its mark. She pulled herself back to her feet when the net covered her.

"Not now," she spat.

Nightbreaker cut into her right wing as the net weighed her down. The second spear took her in the stomach. Her healing magic flared to life inside her, but she couldn't do much until the spears were removed. Dropping Nightbreaker, Ren reached for the spear in her wing first, yanking it loose. Before she could grab it, the other Demons were upon her, hacking with fresh blades.

Fire burst to life from the palms of Ren's hands, burning through the net and scorching her attackers. Still, they kept on, and she suddenly knew that it wouldn't be enough. She had pushed herself too hard these past few days. Rella and Teo jumped to her defense, each trying to disarm one of the Demons quickly. Divinity let out a ferocious roar and sprang onto the back of one of the pair.

Ren shook off the remainder of the net and yanked the spear from her gut. She cried out in pain as the healing magic began to take hold. While one hand clamped onto the bloody hole in her midsection, the other sought for Nightbreaker.

Divinity was thrown to the ground as one of the Demons jumped for the Seraph. It seemed that her death was their only focus. An icicle the size of a spear impaled the creature before it could make it to her. The second demon fell before the blows of the two Balance Monks moments later. Ren slowly stood. Around her, the Demons had been pushed back, and the soldiers and watchmen were forming a solid perimeter.

Tess approached, ice crystals covering the length of her arms.

"How?" was all Ren could muster to say.

"The blood of the goddess," Tess replied.

The commander motioned and another soldier raised his arms. The fallen stones of the wall began to lift and stack themselves on top of the corpse of the Divine Beast. It wouldn't last for long, but at the moment, the wall was repaired enough to stop a further invasion.

"We've taken to calling them Demigods," Edmund said as he approached. "They have been indispensable in our efforts to protect the city from the Demons, and from Castille and his Paladins."

Ren's heart jumped in her chest. She knew that something was wrong in her city beyond the siege. Why had there been no Paladins at the walls? How had the Guardian been awakened? Ren noticed that the defense of the wall seemed to be centered in one of the guard houses ahead. She started walking in that direction and waved for Edmund to follow.

"Tell me everything," she said.

THE CHAIR EXPLODED into a shower of wood and dust.

"I'll kill him before the sun sets!" the Seraph raged.

"My lady," Edmund said, holding his hands up to calm her. "They have blocked themselves into the inner city. We need not worry about them now; the wall needs our attention."

Ren was so taken aback by the brashness of his suggestion that her anger abated. From what little she remembered of the man, he never would have questioned her before. It seemed that holding the city together in her absence had given him more courage than she would have expected.

And who would respect the word of a Seraph now?

"Don't forget the Tempest Born," a strangely familiar voice said from the back of the room.

Ren looked up and saw that the speaker had slipped into the back of the room behind the gathering of City Watch and Demigods. She knew his face instantly: Arkos Lighthammer. So, it seemed there was a Paladin that was working against Castille. But why this one?

Arkos pushed his way forward and nodded casually to Ren.

"Those creatures that Luna made for Castille cannot be ignored. They are made from the bodies of our sacred dead. We must put them to rest. And while Castille has so far kept them in the inner city, I wouldn't count on that to continue once word of your return spreads. He can't risk a challenge to his power. Goddess or not, you are the true Seraph, and many will flee Castille to rejoin you."

"I appreciate your conviction, Arkos," Edmund said flatly, "but I don't expect much from your father's ilk in the inner city. Not any longer."

"Nor do I," Ren said. "Beyond Arkos, how many Paladins do we have to our cause? Surely some returned from the battle at the Rim with you, Tess?"

Tess looked away for a fleeting moment. When she returned the Seraph's gaze, her eyes were flint.

"We have nearly two dozen, my lady. Most didn't make it, and of those who did, over half returned to join Castille in the inner city."

Ren was reminded of the first time she had become aware of Tess, a night on the steps of the Fourth Spire some years ago.

"Your sisters?" she asked.

"Gwen was killed in the battle at the Great Chasm. Ariana is in the inner city, though her allegiance is firmly with us."

"I am sorry for your loss," Ren said, weakly.

Beside the Demigod, Divinity nuzzled at her hand. Perhaps she smelled Arra on her.

"What of the Divine Beasts you brought with you?" Liara, Edmund's second asked.

"Less than we started with, unfortunately. We suffered heavy losses at Seatown..." Ren trailed off. "Four came to the city with me. Several days behind us march the people of Seatown. They come to our aid. We must be ready for them."

Screaming started from outside. It seemed that their respite had come to an end.

The body of a screaming City Watch member flew into the room. He scrambled to his feet just as the pale, winged figure of Rhenaris's Herald walked in behind him.

"You don't have much time," she hissed. "My grip on my own forces is waning. You best make a plan, Seraph. Your doom comes."

14

---

en had been back in her city for days but with the siege going as poorly as it was, it felt as if it had been a lifetime. Already, Trent was joining her parents; a hazy apparition from her past that she chose not to dwell on, lest she falter.

Ren and Edmund looked at a map of the city from the upper level of a shop in the middle ring of the city. While the eastern gatehouse still held for now under the command of Liara, much of the slums had fallen. The walls had been scaled and breached in multiple places. All their Divine Beasts could do for them was prevent their enemy counterparts from making it inside the city, and they were failing at even that whenever Luna's pet got involved.

So far, they had kept Ren's return a secret from the majority of the city. What passed through the citizens and guards who hadn't seen her return was simply rumor. All along the barrier to the inner city stood the immobile forms of the Tempest Born, and for now, they aimed to keep it that way. No doubt Castille knew of her return from the treacherous Luna, but what he could keep from his forces he could pretend didn't exist.

The areas of the slums that had been invaded were evacuated to the middle ring. Looking at the map with its blood-red stains showing where the enemy now held told Ren that this wouldn't last. They needed a true place to fall back to. And they needed a miracle to turn the tide of this battle.

A member of the Watch knocked at the door. Edmund answered and exchanged whispers with the woman before returning. Ren gave him a quizzical glance. Even though she was in charge, the captain still kept his fair share of secrets.

"Elise," Edmund said, clearing his throat awkwardly. "I promised Trent that I would keep her safe. She is also watching a boy named Ajax who is under my care. So far, her hovel is outside of the fighting, but I fear that it won't be for long. My efforts to move her have proven to be… inadequate."

"Where would you move her?" Ren asked.

"Back here for now, until we find a more permanent place."

"Show me where it is and I will speak to her. She needs to hear of her son…"

THE SERAPH LANDED in the street in front of the small home where Trent had grown up. Over the last few days, she hadn't flown anywhere lest she be seen. After looking at the map of the city, she was beginning to doubt that it mattered. Either the Tempest Born would come off the walls of the inner city looking for her, or her people would find themselves smashed against them as they fled from the Demons and Accursed.

She steeled herself for the conversation ahead. This would be worse than any she had since returning to this city. Trent had often spoken of the cantankerous old woman who had raised him. Ren hadn't thought of being the one to tell her that her adopted son had perished. Nor that she and Trent had shared a short but passionate love these last few weeks.

Did he ever talk about me to her? When he came to visit with Devin, did he blush and mention his affections? Why does it matter now?

Ren swallowed hard. Nothing about this seemed to make sense to her. She was a little girl again. It was almost as if Trent was bringing her home to meet his mother. Why? He was dead, and she was leading a city in the middle of a siege. Chances were that she and everyone else in this city would be dead within the fortnight.

The knock at the door was short and curt. Nothing about this meeting was going according to plan and it hadn't even happened yet. Ren could hear the distant sounds of battle; the cries of the dead and the dying. Her city was falling while she cowered on the doorstep of some old woman.

"I already told you people that—" Elise grumped as she opened the door.

The old woman's pronouncement died on her lips as she looked up at the Seraph. Ren had to catch her as she started to fall backward.

"The Lady Ren," she stammered. "You have returned."

In the back of the hovel, a small child began to cry.

"Elise," Ren began as she helped the woman stand. "I'm not sure where to begin—"

"Trent! Where is Trent? If you have returned, then surely he has come with you."

Ren felt the tears welling up again. This time she didn't fight them.

"Trent fought bravely with me, and for his valor, he was also made a Seraph. He perished fighting Divine Beasts at Seatown. I loved him and I couldn't keep him safe. Forgive me."

To Ren's surprise, the old woman pulled her close. Elise's frail frame was wracked with sobs, yet Ren felt a strength in her still.

They stood that way for a long time. It was almost as if the siege had paused for them to grieve.

"My lady," Elise finally choked out. "Would you have died for him if you had been given the chance?"

"Without question," Ren whispered.

"Then in a way, I am glad that he died fighting. My Trent carried too much pain with him. He didn't need another ghost to weigh him down along with Terric. Perhaps this was the High God's mercy. Why have you come, surely not just to break the heart of an old woman?"

Ren wiped her eyes before answering, "No. In fact, I have come to get you. I know you have spurned the attempts of Edmund to protect you at Trent's request, but I ask that you do not ignore mine."

Elise scrunched up her face into a wrinkled scowl.

"Where in this city is safe, my lady? The enemy has breached the walls. Where would you have me go?"

"We have not given up hope yet."

"Nor should you, but I ask again, what place is safer for me and the boy than any other? If I have to choose a place to die, I'd rather do it in the home that raised Trent and Terric."

"The inner city," Ren said, an idea taking shape. "We will not give them access to the Cathedral."

"THIS IS MADNESS," Edmund said. "We can't fight on two fronts."

"I like it," Arkos laughed.

Tess simply nodded in agreement.

"Our only hope is to fall back to the inner city. If we can get the majority of our people in there, we don't have to worry about them while we fight in the streets. If we don't take the inner city now, our people will be smashed against Castille's wall."

"With all due respect," Edmund began, "you are letting your

personal vendetta get in the way of strategy. We have yet to see the Tempest Born in action, and they have a small army of Paladins and a Seraph! It's too risky. Our best hope is to pull back to the middle ring and try and push the bastards out, block by block, until Seatown arrives."

"We don't have the time for that," Ren said. "Our Herald told us as much when I arrived days ago. Her forces are nearing the breaking point. At this point, we don't even know if they are still out there."

"Reconnaissance outside the wall says they are gone," Tess said.

The room murmured in disapproval. Ren had dispatched a Divine Beast to each breach earlier that morning, but they had already fallen back to rest. The Guardian hadn't been seen since the night before.

"I'll take no further debate. Nor do I expect you to blindly send your men to their deaths, Captain," Ren said. "I will not allow any to stand in the way of keeping the people of this city safe, but I won't expect you to blindly follow my orders. The world has changed. Being the Seraph of Illux isn't what it was when I left. Illux is as much yours to command as it is mine. For this reason, I will be attacking Castille's forces with Arkos, Tess, and her Demigods. I will let you dispatch your people where you see fit."

She let the last pronouncement hang in the air. Finally, Edmund nodded and began barking out orders to the members of the City Watch. Orders to prepare an evacuation into the inner city. Ren raised an eyebrow at him.

"I'm coming with you. I was a guest of Castille for quite some time while you were away. He has much to answer for."

"Good," Ren said. "Tess, prepare your people. We attack within the hour."

. . .

A Seraph, a Paladin, two Balance Monks, the Captain of the City Watch, and several dozen Demigods marched down one of the main roads into the inner city. They made no attempt to hide their approach. They needed to take one of the main gates quickly, so that as many people could flee to the inner city as possible. Tess and the rest of her people were stationed at another gate, just waiting to see if the appearance of Ren would draw most of the enemy, allowing her force to easily take that gate as well.

Ahead, the forms of the Tempest Born loomed above the gate. Their metallic bodies glistened in the midday sun. Each held a sword in one hand and a shield in the other. They were like dead reflections of real Paladins. The sight made Ren's skin crawl.

Luna, you will pay for defiling our heroes this way.

The goddess didn't respond.

A more human shape moved on the wall above the gathered force.

"Halt! In the name of Castille, Seraph of Illux, who approaches the inner gate?" he shouted.

"The rightful Seraph, come to take back her city from a usurper!" Arkos shouted in reply.

"There is only one Seraph!" the man yelled again. "And he sits in the Fourth Spire!"

Ren sprang into the air, landing in front of the Paladin before he could draw his weapon.

"Think again," she said.

The Paladin's head fell in front of the gate with a wet crunch, his crumpled body following soon after. The Tempest Born sprung to life, attacking the Seraph with fluid strokes. They didn't hesitate, even as Nightbreaker savagely met them blow for blow.

Below, Arkos and the others shouted and sprang into action, scaling the wall with hooks and ladders that they had hidden in the nearby buildings. Ren noticed that Edmund was up first, and just as quickly he slipped down the other side to get the gate open.

Ren knocked the blade from the hand of the nearest Tempest Born. The gleaming skull showed no change of expression. She raised Nightbreaker overhead and brought the blade down on her adversary. It blocked her blow with its shield, now held in both hands. Even a Paladin would have been knocked backward by the strength of her arm. Ren attacked again, this time rending the shield in two. The skeletal figure discarded it and jumped onto her, wrapping its cold fingers around her throat.

Nothing showed in its eye sockets save a faint blue glow. Ren tried to push the thing off, but it held fast. She slipped her hands onto its face and bathed it in flame. Still, the creature squeezed her neck until her vision began to fade. Then she screamed, and the intensity of the fire flowing from her hands became white hot. The metal on the Tempest Born began to glow orange and red. A blow from behind caved in its now brittle skull.

Arkos pulled Ren to her feet just as the gate below her began to open. Around her, the small amount of Tempest Born had all been destroyed, but several Demigods lay dead. This would not be easy, but what choice did they have?

Further into the inner city, Ren noticed a battalion of the silver monstrosities marching toward them. They had gained their first foothold into Castille's sanctum, but at what cost?

15

"**G**ods," Brandon cursed.

Ahead, they could see the City of Illux, its glittering walls surrounded by a tide of darkness. More than one plume of smoke rose from behind the wall. Even from this distance, it was clear that they were too late. The walls of the city had been breached.

Admiral Wyn road up beside Trent.

"What now, Seraph?" She asked. "The Lady Ren promised me that we would not engage if it was a fool's errand. I see no way that our people can make a difference here. It looks as if the city has already fallen."

We can't be too late. There must be a way...

Trent shaded his eyes and looked up at Aenna, begging for some kind of sign. He would fly ahead, alone if need be. But if he could get more people into the city, maybe they would have a chance to repel the invading force. The field before the city was littered with corpses, after all. The Forces of Darkness had taken heavy losses to get into Illux. Perhaps there was hope yet.

"Wait for my signal," he said, finally. "Let me fly ahead and take stock of the situation. I will hold true to Ren's word; if there is no hope or no safe passage, I will not expect your people to march to their deaths."

Wyn nodded and spurred her horse back toward her people. "Prepare yourselves!" She shouted.

Trent looked to his father and Gil before taking to the air. As he winged his way toward the city he passed over thousands of bodies of Demons and Accursed. Other corpses were strewn about in less number as well: the twisted remains of the soldiers who had knelt before the Herald, and the occasional Divine Beast. This far out there seemed to be no sign of the Forces of Light.

How could we have killed this much of the enemy without suffering any losses ourselves?

Ahead, dark shapes flitted back and forth above the walls of the city. More than one Divine Beast was preparing to dive down to the streets below. Steeling himself for a battle, Trent tightened his grip on Godtaker and dove for the nearest breach in the wall. Shouts rose up from below followed by the errant crossbow-bolt or a blast of flame. He dodged these with ease as he swooped lower to get a better grasp of the situation.

The streets of the slums near this breach were chaos. Demons and Accursed ran rampant, pillaging homes and cutting down men and women caught in the open. And yet there was still an organized resistance. Volleys of arrows from the rooftops and along the wall cut down the invaders. Stones flew through the air, followed by walls of swords, gusts of wind, and cyclones of flame. It almost seemed as if the power of the gods themselves was defending the city.

If I could find a way to get the army a path into the city...

A clawed foot batted Trent out of the air. He punched through the thatched roof of a house and landed on a wooden table, shattering it. Through the Seraph-sized hole in the ceiling he could make out the shape of a large Divine Beast descending toward him. It had the body of a lion, with the head of an eagle and gigantic wings to match. He recognized this Divine Beast from tapestries in the Fourth Spire: The Guardian of Illux.

"It must have me confused with a Herald," he grumbled.

Trent flew back through the hole and approached the Divine Beast with his hands raised.

"I am a Seraph!" He shouted over the din of the fighting. "My name is Trent! I come with the Lady Ren!"

"Traitors!" The Guardian boomed.

"What?"

Trent ducked its claw this time. It opened its mouth and a gout of white flame erupted toward him. He dropped beneath it, raising Godtaker to rake its belly.

No.

Trent circled around again, sheathing his sword.

"This was the blade of Arra!" He yelled. "I will not use it against one of her champions!"

The Guardian stopped short, its wing beats reminding Trent of Akklor. He shivered but didn't break his gaze. Something horrible had happened in Illux, but he would not allow them to kill each other while the true enemy invaded.

"The Seraph and Luna have told me of your treachery. Samson and Ren have turned against the Light. They brought my brothers and sisters here to conquer what was left when the Gods of Darkness are done with their siege. I will speak no further words to your ilk!"

Its mouth opened again for another barrage. Trent held fast, neither drawing his blade nor using his magic as a shield.

"Think! The people of Illux die below us. *Our* people! How can you worry about traitors when a common enemy stains our streets with our blood? The last time the servants of the enemy breached the walls of Illux while you slept, my own brother was slain before my very eyes. We fight the same enemy."

The Guardian paused, its breath retreating back into its throat.

"Our people…" The Guardian trailed off. "I have been asked to ignore them. To fall back to the inner city and dispatch the heretical Seraph. But this was not my purpose…"

"The people of Seatown have marched to our aid. Do the other Divine Beasts still live?"

"They do, I have not killed any of my brethren…"

"Find them, clear a path so that the army can make it inside the city," Trent said. "There is still hope."

"Hope," The Guardian said. "Yes. I was created for hope."

The Divine Beast turned and flew toward the southern end of the city. Trent hoped that his words had been enough. It seemed that the Light had truly fractured since he had been separated from Ren. Time was short, and what little hope he claimed was left would soon flee if he didn't act.

Trent turned to fly back toward the army when he saw a familiar shape heading in his direction. Tyr hung in the air beside him.

"The High God smiles upon us," the Divine Beast said. "Your return surely heralds a change in the tide for this city. See to it that the eastern gate is opened, Lord Trent. We will clear a path for your army".

Trent nodded. He scanned below for the gatehouse. It seemed to still be defended by the City Watch. Hopefully, they wouldn't take much convincing to open the gates with so much of the enemy still milling about outside. Tyr was right; the breach in the wall was too choked with corpses and rubble for the Seatown army to be able to make it inside before the majority of them were slaughtered from the rear.

Trent landed in front of the building as the shapes of multiple Divine Beasts flew overhead. Already white and blue flames bathed the world outside the wall. The people of Seatown needed to be ready. A path was being cleared for them.

A dark shape crawled over the top of the wall, barely avoiding the flames below. It was another Divine Beast and not one of theirs. The creature was covered in a black carapace, with claws and stingers that made it resemble a giant scorpion. It came right for the gatehouse, skittering along the top of the wall. Trent wouldn't have time to battle it and communicate with the City Watch—

A golden form slammed into the Divine Beast howling with a deafening roar.

"Guod!" Aion shouted. "You will not gain entrance to my city!"

The golden ape beat his chest before slamming his fists into the creature it had named Guod. Their blows shook the wall and nearly dropped Trent to his knees. The battle the Divine Beasts had been created for had finally arrived.

"Open the gate!" Trent shouted. "Open the gate! Seatown comes to our aid!"

The Seraph ran through the confused throng of City Watch. Many stared at him in awe. More Demons and Accursed filled the breach, quickly pressing against them. Trent had no time to stop and help. By now the people of Seatown would be running through the path of corpses made for them. He couldn't leave them outside lest the Forces of Darkness regroup and slaughter them.

"Open the Gate!"

Trent reached the gatehouse door just as black lightning wrapped his body and threw him into the wall. One of his wings had been broken at an odd angle, and he felt the flesh in multiple places was burned. The blood-red form of a Herald stood in front of the gatehouse glaring at him. Trent's healing magic flared to life, mending his wing and flesh.

The Herald disappeared inside the gatehouse before Trent could stand. Screams followed. Overhead, Aion cried out in pain as he was struck by one of Guod's stingers. Trent swallowed and pushed himself up. He wasn't done healing, but there was no time.

Ahead, the door to the gatehouse hung ajar. Before he was inside, Trent could already make out the stains of blood that coated the floors and walls.

Trent shoved the door the rest of the way open and stepped inside. Gore and viscera coated nearly every surface. Dozens of members of the City Watch had been torn to shreds already. Above, Trent could hear more screaming. He needed to open the gate, but he couldn't leave more people to die.

It will be even worse if I attack this Herald.

He moved to the back of the gatehouse and found the mechanism to open the gate. The men and women who had been guarding it were nothing more than a collection of limbs. Trent tried not to wretch as he gripped the wheel, slick with blood, and began to turn. What normally would have taken a team was easily accomplished by one with Divine Blood. Outside the gate slowly ground open. Once the wheel would turn no longer, Trent ran up the stairs to the higher levels, but he knew that he was already too late.

At the top of the gatehouse, Trent found a circle of corpses gathered around one woman. The Herald sprang from the window moments later, winging its way back into the city. The woman at the center of the circle still drew ragged breaths, though she was missing both arms. Trent rushed to her side placing his hands behind her head. It was too late to save her, even with the magic that he possessed—still, he filled her with what healing magic he could spare, hoping to ease her passing to the Astral Plane.

"Another Seraph," she choked. "Fuck me, what a day."

"I'm sorry," Trent said. "I tried to get here in time, but I needed to open the gate. Reinforcements are here. Go to your rest knowing that Illux will not fall."

"Tell Edmund," she sputtered, "that Liara said he was a damned good captain."

Then she was still. Trent lowered her to the floor. Scarlet

stained his armor and hair. Yet there was still work to be done. He followed the Herald out the window and flew through the open gate to the plains beyond.

The path from the city to the army was a smoldering line of corpses. On either side, Divine Beasts continued to fly the perimeter, creating two walls of white and blue flames that kept the Forces of Darkness from harassing the army. Lythe flew the length of the tunnel, breathing ice onto the larger smoldering patches to keep the humans safe when they crossed.

Trent quickly reached the front of the army where Gil and Wyn led the brisk march. They would need to run soon if they wanted to make it into the city alive.

"You certainly know how to keep a bargain!" Wyn shouted.

"Aye!" Trent replied. "I swore to keep this city safe as well, and I aim to do just that. Now we must hurry. Dozens died to get this gate open."

Wyn screamed for her forces to run. The ragged army from Seatown began sprinting down the tunnel of flames into the open gates of Illux. The heat of the flames was nearly overwhelming, but so far it was keeping the enemy at bay. Only a few more moments were needed...

Ahead, Aion let out a cry louder than any he had before. Trent's eyes snapped up and saw the golden Divine Beast's hands wrapped around Guod. The stingers of the creature were embedded in the chest of the ape. Both combatants fell from the wall.

"No!" Trent cried out.

Aion and Guod landed on the right side of the tunnel, their corpses extinguishing the flames. In moments Demons sprang into the opening, trying to block off the army from entering the gate.

"Weapons!" Trent shouted. "Don't slow!"

Without warning the Guardian of Illux landed in front of them, batting the Demons aside. The gryphon jumped onto the corpse of his one-time friend, bathing the outside of the tunnel with more heavenly flame. Trent and the others rushed past and finally entered the chaos that was Illux.

Trent turned to make for the gatehouse and closed the gates behind them. It was engulfed in flames, the last shattered resistance of the City Watch were fleeing from the Demons and Accursed that pushed this way. For a moment Trent felt as if he had led these people to their doom. He gripped Godtaker tighter and felt Arra within him.

"To the inner city! We must get out of the slums!"

Gil and Wyn led the army down the main road, only slowing when they met scattered resistance. The further they made it away from the wall the fewer Demons they encountered. Trent brought up the rear with his father, waiting for the surviving Divine Beasts to join them. The Seraph lanced white-hot fire down the blade of Godtaker into any of the Demons that dared get too close.

The Divine Beasts entered the city. The Guardian came last. He stood upon his hind legs and blasted the upper wall with a massive gout of flame. Moments later the wall collapsed, blocking the enemy from following them.

Trent could see that the others were mourning the loss of Aion. He needed to channel their grief and rage in the right direction, or he risked losing more of them.

"We must fall back to the inner city! We have to find Ren!"

"I cannot follow you, Seraph," the Guardian said. "Aion's death is my fault. I failed each of you. I will seek my own death in defense of this city."

"If you seek penance, then come with me and take the fight to those who misled you," Trent said.

The Guardian let out a roar.

"Yes. Castille will pay for this, and Luna if she is to show herself on this plane again! We will cover the retreat to the inner city and then join you there."

Castille.

Trent gripped Godtaker.

Of course this goes back to Castille.

Out of the corner of his eye Trent caught sight of a red blur heading towards his army. There was one foe he needed to deal with before finding Ren.

16

The Tempest Born continued to march toward them, unhindered by the few losses that they had sustained. Ren and the Demigods sent multiple barrages of magical energies into the steel automatons but to no avail. When they finally got closer, Teo, Rella, and Arkos sprang into action, striking the skeletal warriors with a flurry of blows before quickly falling back, lest they find themselves surrounded and pulled down.

Edmund tried to regain control of his nerves, but it was no use. Even Demons and Accursed had flesh and blood, but these *things*? Luna and Castille had created something far more inhuman and dangerous than the Gods of Darkness had ever dreamed of. He knew that there were hundreds of Tempest Born in the inner city, and they were currently struggling to get past mere dozens.

Gods, I should have gone back to the wall.

He looked around for something that they could use to their advantage. On either side of the now-paved street, there were two modest mansions with ornate hanging gardens and small stone walls. If they fled into one of those they might have a chance to survive longer. That would mean that they were trapped again. That would mean that they never reached the Grand Cathedral.

Then an idea took hold.

"My lady!" he called out.

Ren heaved a Tempest Born into several of its fellows, knocking the lot of them to the ground. She turned and flew back closer to the guard captain.

"If we get inside one of the mansions we can pull it down on top of them!" Edmund said. "That will give us time to get out the back and run deeper into the city!"

Ren smiled.

"Everyone!" She shouted. "Follow Edmund!"

Edmund turned and ran into the left mansion. The others quickly followed behind him. Arkos left the foyer for a moment before returning with a large table that he used to barricade the door. Overhead they could hear the loud thump indicating that Ren had flown through one of the upper windows.

"What in the High God's name is going on here?" a voice shouted.

Edmund spun to see an older man with a wispy beard standing in one of the inner doorways. He had an armful of papers and some gold and silver jewelry. Though frail, the man seemed to project an arrogance typical of inner city families.

"I say again, what is happening here? Why are you in my house?"

"We need to get out the back, and quickly!" Edmund hissed. As if to punctuate his words, the door shook on its hinges.

Ren came downstairs, Nightbreaker still clutched in her hand.

"None are upstairs. Where is your family?" she asked the man.

"Traitors, all of you!" He spat.

Arkos walked up to the man grabbing him by the throat.

"Did they do it, you coward? Did they?" The Paladin shouted.

The man couldn't choke out a reply before Arkos broke his

neck. Arkos dropped the man to the floor and looked around the room. To Edmund, it seemed that there was a touch of madness in his eyes. The captain was reminded of a series of inner city murders that he was never able to solve. The Balance Monk named Rella tried to step forward but Teo held her fast.

It can't be.

"We aren't here to kill them all!" Ren chastised. "Why did you do that?"

"With all due respect, my lady," Arkos replied calmly, "the families of the inner city have oppressed Illux for far too long, and you have ignored it. They have corrupted the City Watch, the Church, and now even our sacred dead. If all of them burned it would be a mercy. A few days ago I found out that a group of inner city families, unbeknownst to Castille, planned to use the catacombs to escape the city.

"They aimed to use the people of the slums as a distraction while they scurried to safety like the rats they are. I wouldn't be surprised if half of the homes we find to be empty. Castille and my father are too busy with the distractions of their heresy to realize that the very people they claim to rule are abandoning them!"

The door cracked under the strain of the Tempest Born assault. A window shattered as a silver head poked through staring at its prey.

"We don't have time for this!" Edmund shouted.

Another crack signaled that the door was finally broken. The group followed Ren out the back of the mansion into the garden just as the Tempest Born made it inside. Edmund swallowed. He hoped that his plan would work.

"Bring it down!"

One of the Demigods closed their eyes and placed their palms flat upon the ground. The earth began to shake violently. Edmund lost his footing but found himself caught by Teo. The monk merely nodded. The mansion, and a few other nearby buildings, collapsed into a pile of rubble. Without waiting to see if his plan had worked, the group turned and continued toward the Grand Cathedral.

As they ran ahead they didn't find any further signs of Tempest Born. Several of the houses sat empty, their doors hanging ajar. It was an eerie sight to Edmund. Even the slums in the midst of the siege had more life than this.

It seemed that Arkos was right. Even after the miracle of a new Seraph. Even after the Tempest Born. Even after a literal goddess appeared before them, many of the families of the inner city were so selfish and cowardly that they would attempt to flee Illux and leave everyone else to die.

Let them go. They aren't worth the rest of us dying over.

Soon they were close. The five spires of the Grand Cathedral loomed overhead. Arkos stopped running and looked down another street. Ren and the others turned to see what he was doing. Somehow, Edmund already knew.

"I have business to attend to at Lighthammer Manor. With your leave, my lady," he said.

"Go," Ren replied. "May it bring you peace."

Arkos nodded and ran off alone.

"We take back our city, today," Ren said.

"Aye," the group replied.

The Seraph turned and flew ahead. Filled with hope, Edmund and the others quickly followed.

THE INNER PLAZA of Illux was not as empty as the streets leading to it. People milled about in all directions, seemingly without purpose. More than one siege weapon was under construction near the cathedral. Paladins drilled in the training yard as if the world wasn't ending, and Tempest Born stood in small battalions scattered around the plaza like silent sentinels.

In front of the Grand Cathedral, Edmund saw that the statues of both Arra and Samson had been pulled down. His breath caught in his throat. The collapse of their entire faith was nearly absolute. Castille had destroyed over a thousand years of religion in a few short days, and the people of the inner city had followed along without question. On the far side of the plaza opened a cavernous hole to the catacombs from whence the Guardian had emerged.

A gibbet stood near the Paladin barracks. Dozens of bloated corpses were on display. Edmund clenched his fists as he looked at Ren. Her face was contorted into a snarl the like of which he had never seen on her before.

People then took notice of them. Some pointed and cried out, others ran.

"The lady has returned!" one shouted. "We are being punished for our blasphemy!"

Ren unsheathed Nightbreaker.

"Spare them if you can," she growled. "Kill only Castille and the Paladins."

Across the plaza, more shouting started as an explosion of fire and stone rocked the crowd. Flashes of blue were followed by shards of ice throwing Tempest Born into the air. Tess and the others had arrived,

Edmund didn't wait for orders. He pulled his sword free and charged ahead shouting, "For Illux!"

The others followed him while Ren flew ahead. The people of the inner city fled before them without any resistance. Tempest Born sprang to life, lifting blades and marching toward them methodically. Edmund ducked past them and kept running. He would leave those monsters to the Demigods. His quarry was at the Cathedral.

A foolish man drew an ornate sword and tried to stop Edmund. Not all of them were cowards, it seemed. The Captain of the City Watch caught the man by the wrist with his free hand and gutted him with his sword. Brave or not, he was dead.

By now the Paladins had stopped practicing and begun running towards the two contingents of Demigods. Edmund searched among the faces for the one he wanted but at this distance, they all looked the same.

What am I doing? How in the High God's name can I hope to kill a Paladin?

He reached the steps of the cathedral, its doors already closed and barred. The two Paladin guards flared blue magic in their hands. If he didn't move quickly he would be little more than ash on the ground. Then he knew what he had to do.

"Yan!" Edmund shouted.

He ducked behind a nearby pile of material that was probably going to be used to create another ballista. The blue flames slammed into the wood and stone, bathing Edmund in heat and debris. He looked around again but still didn't see his quarry. Beside him was a long coil of rope that he grabbed and tucked under his arm.

"Yan!" he shouted again.

The guardsman ducked and sprinted away as another blast of flame struck his hiding place.

"Stupid!" he cursed.

He reached his target, one of the siege weapons that appeared to be functional. It was already loaded and pointed away from the cathedral toward the outer wall. Dropping his sword, he slammed his shoulder into it. Its wheels slowly turned as the man and machine groaned in unison. Another blast of fire came toward him, but thankfully this one missed.

When it was in position, Edmund kicked the lever and released his missile. The giant spear slammed into the door of the Grand Cathedral, exploding inward. The two Paladin guards were thrown out of the way by the collision.

"Yan!" Edmund shouted again.

He grabbed another large spear and began loading the weapon.

These hadn't been designed to be operated by teams smaller than three. That meant that Edmund was going to be far slower and more vulnerable than he should have been. He hoped this would still work. Once the spear was in place he tied the rope to the lever and his left leg as insurance. With any luck, it would be long enough to get him to the doorway.

Behind him, he could hear the din of the battle. He wasn't sure, but he thought he could make out the sound of Ren's voice shouting over the cacophony. If nothing else, at least he opened the Grand Cathedral for her.

"Yan!" He shouted again.

Ahead of him, the two Paladins were beginning to stand. A strong hand grabbed him by the back of the neck and lifted him into the air.

"You are a larger fool than I thought possible!" Yan shouted.

The Paladin threw Edmund to the ground at the base of the stairs. It felt like his arm broke when he landed. Trying to ignore the pain and the other two Paladins, Edmund began pulling himself up the steps.

"He's mine," Yan said from behind him. "Go help the others subdue that bitch."

Edmund ignored him and kept climbing. Just as he reached the doorway he felt a heavy boot press on his back. Yan used his foot to roll Edmund over. His expression was one of contempt. His hand rested on the pommel of his sword.

"Tell me one thing," he said through a smile. "Why in the High God's name would you come back?"

"Because," Edmund said as he pulled the rope taught. "You need to learn consequences."

Yan's last expression was one of confusion.

17

rkos Lighthammer looked upon his ancestral home for what he knew would be the last time. The towering facade of white stone with blue accents and gold filigree was lifeless and hollow. What he had expected had come to pass; his family must have fled to the catacombs.

The front door was still ajar. No servants greeted him as he walked into the foyer. He wondered if they had been allowed to escape with his family, or if they had been left to die with the rest of the people from the slums. The thought sickened him either way. They were good people and didn't deserve to die, nor did he like the idea of them being abused by his father somewhere outside the city where they had no chance at choosing another life.

He entered into the great hall and was surprised to see a fire in one of the hearths. The Lighthammer no longer hung above the mantle but was instead lying across the lap of a seated figure that he knew to be his father. The Lighthammer patriarch sat in one of his ornate chairs, staring at the fireplace, his back to his son. Even so, the man tensed as the Paladin entered.

"Arkos," he said. "I've been waiting for you to come crawling back for some time."

Arkon stood, gripping the Lighthammer in one hand. His eyes reflected the fire from the hearth as he turned to face his son.

"Father," Arkos said, "where are the others? Did they follow your plan and flee into the catacombs?"

"They did. And once we are done here, I will join them."

Arkos moved further into the room, his hand sitting on the pommel of his sword.

"Even for you, that is cowardly," Arkos spat. "After Castille even made you an undeserved Paladin, you choose to abandon him?"

Arkon bristled at the accusation. "I am doing what I have always done: protecting the future of this family! Even with the Tempest Born Illux is doomed. Now that the bitch Ren has returned, I expect the inner city to fall to the invaders within the day."

He might be right. But I won't abandon this city. Not again.

"Where will you go?"

"Seatown perhaps. Or the Rim. It matters not. We will escape and the Lighthammer name will live on."

Arkos laughed. "That must irritate you to no end to see your last male heir stay behind then. Even if our name continues, it won't be through you. A lesser branch, as you call it."

Then it was Arkon who laughed. "Your mother may be beyond child-bearing years, but I do not plan to give up on my seed so easily."

"So what now, then?" Arkos asked, "why did you wait for me?"

Arkon gripped the warhammer with both hands.

"I wanted to rid this family of the last stain on its honor. A traitor and a murderer will carry my name no longer."

"So you do know?"

"Aye," Arkon spat. "You were the one killing the inner city fami-lies. You were the Whitestone Killer."

Arkos held back a chuckle. He always found the name that the City Watch had given him to be rather droll. He pulled his sword free.

"Then you really are a coward. You could have turned me in at any time and you didn't to protect yourself. Good thing I came back then, there is one family that has escaped justice for too long."

Arkos lept at his father, sword raised. Arkon swung the Lighthammer in a wide arc. He was too slow and Arkos was upon him before the blow could connect. His sword bit into the shoulder of his father when a blast of fire sent him flying backward.

The Lighthammer patriarch howled in pain, smashing his chair with the hammer. Bits of wood and fabric exploded around the hall, some making it into the fire. He lurched toward his son with a fury that Arkos didn't know his father possessed. Even so, he had no experience being a Paladin, no real combat training, all he possessed was arrogance.

Arkos jumped to his feet, lighting the tapestries and curtains around the hall as he did so. In a matter of moments, the light of his blue flame was replaced by the red and orange of the fires that were already beginning to engulf the manor.

Acrid smoke twisted about the hall, making the form of his charging father hazy and surreal. The old man lunged out of the smoke swinging the Lighthammer down with a savage force. Arkos rolled out of the way before slicing upward, disabling his father's left arm. He could see the faint glow of the healing magic that sprung to life in Arkon's wounds.

It wouldn't make a difference.

Arkos slammed his father with his shoulder, sending the older man sprawling. The Lighthammer skittered away into the smoke.

I wish I had the time to enjoy this.

"You see this?" Arkos asked as he stuck his blade into his father's gut. "This blood that pours out of you? It is the same blood that flows in my veins! You know what that means? It means we are both Lighthammers."

He pulled the sword free and prepared to stab the man again, but his father caught it, his fingers clawing at the blade. Light flashed the sword shattered as Arkos was once again thrown back into the smoke.

"Being a Lighthammer is an honor!" his father shouted. "A privilege!"

"Being a Lighthammer doesn't mean a fucking thing!" Arkos yelled into the inferno. "We aren't any better than anyone else!"

Arkon sprang from the smoke, blood still dripping from his wound. His face was a snarl as he landed on his son, laying blow after blow upon his face. Arkos didn't defend himself this time. His own words began to cut into him. He wasn't any better than anyone else. He was a murderer, even if those he killed deserved it. He wasn't half the man his cousin had been. He wasn't anything other than a rebellious son who inflicted the hatred of his father onto the world around him. Maybe they both deserved to die?

Arkos kicked his father in the groin and pushed him off. Around them, the manor was completely engulfed in flames. While the masonry held for the moment, every scrap of cloth and piece of furniture was fuel for the raging inferno. Soon nothing would be left of the Lighthammer estate save a smoldering ruin. It was fitting that both men die here.

As if by divine providence, the smoke cleared before him and he saw the Lighthammer. Its smooth white and gold surface reflected the red and black of the fire that surrounded it. The Paladin grabbed the hammer and turned to see his father standing behind him.

"You have committed grievous sins, Arkon Lighthammer," Arkos said. "You will now face punishment. Once again the Lighthammer will mete out justice."

His father raised his hands to lance more magical fire into him.

Not one strike of the magic gave Arkos pause. With each blow from the hammer, his father crumpled more and more into the ground. By the time Arkos was done there wasn't much left that resembled a man. The smoke burned his lungs and he felt himself losing consciousness.

Slowly he dropped to his knees to accept his fate. He hoped that even for all of his sins he would find his cousin again.

Forgive me, Devin.

As the darkness overtook him, a grey shape appeared out of the smoke holding out a hand. His cousin had come for him.

18

"Protect the unarmed!" Gil shouted over the clamor.

The crush of the battle pressed against him on all sides. Seatown warriors and unarmed citizens of the slums tried to press forward in a desperate throng toward the safety promised by the inner city. This was madness. The Forces of Darkness had fully breached the walls, and now everyone who wasn't instantly butchered was running in the same direction.

Gil and Wyn fought side by side, hacking away at the Accursed that harried their progress. Demons fought Paladins in the side streets around them, flashes of red and blue illuminating the smoky malaise that hung over the city.

We aren't going to make it.

Gil's thoughts were bleak. Overhead he saw Trent disappear after the scarlet Herald. He grimaced. While a Seraph and a Herald were evenly matched, he didn't want to risk seeing his friend sacrifice himself again. Brandon, Trent's father, shoved his way through a group of Accursed and bolted down an alley in pursuit of his son. High God willing his presence wouldn't put Trent in even more danger.

Facing down the Accursed was like looking at a twisted version of himself. Their ragged husks were not unlike what Gil imagined himself to look like. Each blade-hand that rose against him was met by his own. He shuddered. What had he become?

Admiral Thacker decapitated one of the corpse warriors as it shambled too close to Gil's undefended side. Gil nodded in thanks before scanning further down the road. The inner city was still some ways off, and a crowd of this size could only run so fast. The street shook as a Divine Beast was driven to the ground a few blocks away. Several of the hovels around them collapsed, burying friend and foe alike in the rubble. This slowed the pursuit of the Accursed to a crawl.

That gave Gil an idea.

"Wyn!" he shouted. "Keep them heading farther in. I'll take some archers and we will slow the bastards down!"

She nodded and pushed her way forward toward the front of the Seatown force. As she moved ahead several fighters armed with bows moved back to stay with Gil.

"Keep moving!" she screamed. "Do you want to make it back to the sea or not?"

Gil let the crowd filter around him, leaving him and the archers standing mostly alone in the partially destroyed street. He lanced fire down his sword-arm into the buildings on either side. At first, nothing more happened besides the air getting choked with roiling smoke. After his third attempt, however, a multi-story building collapsed into the road. The rubble wouldn't stop them for long, but every moment counted.

The Paladin ran through the malaise, nearly stumbling head-first into an Accursed. He stuck his blade through the thing's head and continued on. He was forced to squint his eyes against the burning smoke. Another Accursed stumbled by, tripping on some of the rubble Gil had created. The Paladin motioned for the archers to spread out into the buildings on either side of the street.

He smashed the fallen Accursed back in with his boot and cut across the rubble, shouldering through a door. Once inside he made for the upper floor, his body already reacting to the magic that he was preparing.

Smoke poured in through the open window in what looked to be a child's bedroom. Gil leaned out and blasted the street below. Cobblestones and other debris flew into the air as the smoke parted for the blue gout of flames. It didn't look as if he had hit any of the invaders. He took a deep breath and scorched another spot; this time when the scene lit up below he saw dozens of Accursed blown apart by his attack. It seemed that they were starting to regroup and cluster together. As soon as the street lit up from his magical blast, a flurry of arrows descended from the smoke and took out those still standing.

Gil gripped the side of the house and attacked the street once again. He could feel his strength waning. If he kept this up he would most likely black out. Once again he saw the forms of Accursed below, and once again they were taken by arrows. This time the creatures seemed more prepared and several bolts from their crude crossbows whizzed up from the street. Gil ducked just in time, but based on the garbled screams he heard from some of the other houses, some of his archers had not been so lucky.

The Paladin prepared to light up the street once again when the red flame from the outstretched hand of a Demon did it for him. Two houses across the way were engulfed and the smoke cleared as the shape of a burning woman fell to the street below.

No wonder they're regrouping.

More flames followed from below and Gil knew that his plan was spent.

"Rejoin the others!" he shouted out the window, though he doubted it mattered. Most of the archers were probably fleeing by that moment.

He sprinted down the steps and almost made it to the open

doorway when he was thrown backward by a gout of Demon fire. The air was knocked from his lungs as he slid down the hard surface of the home's hearth. He sucked in but all he could taste was smoke. Flashes of the burning village of Marna filled his mind. Panic gripped him for the briefest of moments, then it was replaced by rage.

Gil sprang up and slammed into the hulking form of the Demon as it lumbered into the doorway. He shouted curses that were lost in the sound of the screaming from outside. It didn't matter, the creature would feel his anger one way or another.

Rolling off of his enemy, Gil leaped and threw up a defensive barrier as another barrage of magic struck him. Then he was sprinting forward, barreling into the Demon once again just as it regained its footing. He jammed his sword arm up through a gap in its neck and ripped its head from its shoulders. The Demon shuddered and fell to its knees.

Gil turned and ran back through the smoke toward the inner city and the rest of the survivors he had been charged to protect.

When he caught up to them the crowd was milling about in chaos. Demons harried their flanks, pushing them against a small wall that separated the inner city from the rest of Illux. A large gate stood closed, and silver-bodied warriors glared down at them.

What in the High God's name is this?

Gil searched the faces in the crowd of thousands for any sign of Wyn. He might as well have been looking for a specific stone on the cobbled street. He sighed and ran into an alley. Overhead was the hanging garden of what had most likely been the home of a merchant. It was nowhere near as lavish as that of an inner city manse, but it would do. Gil jumped and grabbed onto one of the plants and pulled himself higher. The Paladin repeated this process again and again until he was able to jump to the rooftop of the house. He jumped to the next roof and the next, scanning the faces below for the Admiral.

There she was towards the middle of the crush, vainly shouting orders to both her people and the people of the slums. It didn't look like it was making a difference. They needed to get the people moving again or else the Demons would cause them to break and flee in all directions.

He scanned the wall, looking over the metallic sentinels that watched the carnage. They were wearing the armor of Paladins, but their visages were altogether inhuman and skeletal. He shuddered. Something had soured in this city and he once again feared that he had helped march the people of Seatown to their deaths. People of the slums tried to climb up the walls but the steel Paladins cruelly cut them down before they reached the top.

There has to be a way.

Gil got a running start before jumping from the rooftop. He skidded to a halt just beside one of the watchers. The Paladin swung his sword arm for the thing's neck. It easily parried his attack and knocked him backward with inhuman strength. In the next instant, Gil noticed that there were several of the steel sentinels lying motionless along the wall. It seemed that someone had been able to overpower them at one point.

Ren.

His sense of purpose renewed, Gil pressed on. Unfortunately, he was weakened from the early skirmish with the Demon, and he knew that his reserves of stamina were almost depleted. Even so, the Paladin mustered the strength to slam his foe with a barrage of energy. It staggered backward but didn't falter. Expending the last of his strength, Gil slammed into the creature just as he had with the Demon earlier. It skittered the last little bit and fell from the wall. The metallic crunch it made when it collided with the street below sounded like he had finally done some damage, but he was unsure that he had truly killed it.

Already, several others were converging on him. Just as quickly as his courage was renewed, it was squashed. He turned and jumped into an opening into the crowd below. There was another path into the inner city, one that he had been afraid to take.

Gil pressed his way through the crowd to where he had last seen Admiral Wyn. Finally, he reached her near the center of the rapidly shrinking circle.

"Wyn!" he shouted. "We can't stay here, and we can't fight the things guarding the wall!"

"Tell me something I don't know, Paladin," she spat.

"I know of another way, but none of us are going to like it."

"Spit it out, Gil!"

"We must make for the catacombs. Most people think that the only entrance is under the Grand Cathedral, but Trent and I found several other passages when we were first initiated. There is one not far from here."

Gil thought back to that horrific adventure that had left Broderick Breaksword dead and Gil stationed in the mountains at Rinwaithe. Rella and Devin had been there too, ferreting out a blood cult that had taken root both in the Rim and below Illux. In the very catacombs that he intended to lead them into.

"I'll take whatever you can give us!" she cried. "Quickly, follow the Paladin if we want to get out of here alive!"

Gil shoved back through the crowd in the direction of the secret entrance. Ren had sealed them up after the Paladins had journeyed down there on the heels of a killer who was performing rituals to honor his dark gods in the city. Even so, Gil knew that he would be able to get them in. The hard part would be funneling everyone inside before they were overrun.

He quickly found what he was looking for ahead of them. A small building that looked like it could have been a simple guard shack for the City Watch. Skeletal statues stood at either side of the great door that was chained shut.

Gil nodded at the door and two of Wyn's men hacked the chains off with axes. The Paladin kicked in the door, spilling years of dust and stale air out into the street. Without waiting for the others to follow, Gil entered the room and scanned the floor. Where there had once been a yawning staircase into the underground, there was now nothing but a stone floor and a pile of old torches in the corner. Relying on his memory of what had been there before, Gil hammered the floor with as much fire as he could muster. It wasn't enough. The mortar around the stones glowed red hot, but the floor still remained intact.

Wyn and her soldiers filtered in behind him. She saw what Gil was attempting to do and barked orders again. Outside the people began to scream as the Demons caught up to them once more. Wyn's soldiers attacked the floor with their axes, breaking apart the stones where Gil had weakened the mortar. In a few moments, there was an opening into the darkness beyond.

Gil grabbed the torches and quickly lit them with the last of his strength. The world around him began to spin before a hand from the Admiral steadied him.

"You can't falter yet, Gil," she said. "You still have a promise to keep."

Gil nodded dumbly and moved down into the catacombs. His mind swam with numbness and fatigue. For a moment he thought he could feel the fingers on his missing arm tingling. Suddenly he was back in Marna, facing down the Herald. He blinked away one horror for another. Leading away from him into the blackness was a long tunnel lined with coffins.

"If we head straight this should take us to a larger central cavern. It will be lit there, and the path up to the Grand Cathedral will be clear," he slurred.

"Then we best move quickly," Wyn said. "I fear most of our people will die in the street before they can follow us."

The Paladin half-stumbled and half-ran ahead, his torch the

first to cut into the darkness and reveal the sleeping dead of Illux. For some reason entering the tomb this time unnerved him even more than it had the last. So close to the dead now, and he simply wished to join them.

Devin.

Behind him, the tunnel was filling with the people from above. Somehow they would have to cram thousands into the catacombs if he hoped to fulfill his oath and keep the people of Seatown alive. Shaking off the malaise that threatened to drag him into the final blackness, he pressed on for what seemed like hours. Soon the tunnel behind him was full of people, some of whom wept. Farther back, beyond the torchlight to the rear of the procession screaming began. The echoes of death reached his ears and bounced off of the coffins. The Demons had made it inside.

Suddenly, the tunnel opened up into a wide cavern. This wasn't the central chamber below the Grand Cathedral, but it was close. Gil recognized the familiar shape of the support pillar in the center of the cavern. These were what held the streets above. If the Demons were to attack this weak point, it would cause chaos in the inner city.

Gil blinked and saw Devin flying through the air, facing down a Divine Beast with a smile on his lips. Devin was truly one of the old heroes come to life. The vision faded, but Devin didn't. Gil felt the squeeze of his strong arms and the warmth of his breath upon his neck. The blackness returned at the corners of his vision, but this time, rather than cold, it felt warm.

He approached the pillar and raised his torch, looking at it for any signs of decay. Small cracks ran along its circumference; nothing that would cause it to collapse on its own, but a place to start.

"Wyn," he whispered.

Thankfully, the Admiral was at his side, otherwise, his words would have been lost to the silence of the dead.

"Have your men weaken this pillar. Tell them to focus their blows on the existing cracks. Take your people and follow the left path ahead. Another few minutes of walking and you should be in the central chamber. You will know it by the torchlight. The priests keep it lit. From there the stairs above should be easy to find."

Wyn nodded at her soldiers who began hacking at the pillar as the crowd came rushing in around them.

"Are you not coming with us?" she asked.

"I will bring up the rear. If we don't bring the tunnels down on top of them, we are simply giving the Demons access to our redoubt in the inner city."

The Admiral looked him in the eyes and clasped his forearm.

"Consider your debt paid," she whispered, and then she was gone, shoving into the throngs of fearful people who now needed a direction to run.

Gil slumped against the pillar, allowing the rhythmic sound of ax-on-stone to place him into a state of meditation.

I will look for you by the High God's side.

He swallowed hard and his pulse quickened as his thoughts drifted to his last night with Devin. His lover had been on a ranging mission with Trent to see why the attacks from Demons and Accursed had stopped recently. Little did any of them know that was the calm before the storm, and by the end of it, most of the Mortal Plane would be wiped out.

The hammering from above him finally stopped and the two soldiers also melted into the last bit of the crowd. The people were running now, no doubt meaning that the Demons were near. Gil stood just as the last of the people faded from the view of his solitary torch.

It was eerily silent then. After an indeterminable amount of time, he began to wonder if he had been mistaken. Then he saw it. The torchlight flickered off of the shining onyx armor of a Demon.

Then another. And another. Soon Gil saw that he was surrounded by Demons and he could hear the shuffling feet of hundreds of Accursed behind them. It seemed that they had gathered their forces before plunging headlong into the catacombs. What he had said to Wyn had been right. If he didn't stop them here, then the inner city would be breached.

He turned and looked up at the pillar. Larger cracks ran from floor to ceiling now, and the center of it was pitted with deep holes. He smiled. A sharp pain blossomed in his stomach but he hardly noticed. The Demons and Accursed were spreading to the tunnels that headed toward the Grand Cathedral. He knew that he couldn't heal his new wound. If he did he would lose consciousness. The laughter of a Demon reached his ears, but it sounded as if it was miles away.

Gil finally looked down at the sword sticking into his gut. The Demon had punched through his armor like it was nothing. Scarlet ran out and pooled on the floor beneath them. Gil started laughing too, the sounds mingling together as the torch began to sputter out.

The Paladin slammed his sword arm into the center of the pillar and filled the cavern with a blinding white light. Surprisingly, the blackness that had dogged him since entering the catacombs never returned. Only the warmth of the light remained.

19

The red blur that Trent knew to be the Herald flew off toward another part of the slums. As he followed the creature the streets below him became increasingly familiar. They were getting close to the part of the slums where he had grown up.

Trent suddenly thought of Elise for the first time since he had returned to Illux. Though he had asked Edmund to watch over her, she was still the woman who raised him and he should have returned to her first. Shame overwhelmed him and he turned his path from that of the Herald to the small hovel that he had once called home.

Has father's return truly clouded my mind that much that I would forsake Elise?

Trent landed in the street just in front of where the house had stood. Most of the homes here were smoldering ruins now. His heart sank. What if he had been too late?

The Seraph walked up to the smoking pile of rubble and began to dig. He hoped that he would find nothing, but fear told him that he would find the corpse of a woman too stubborn to leave her home even in the face of annihilation. He swallowed hard and kept digging even as the sound of footsteps approached him from behind.

"Trent," his father wheezed.

Trent turned and looked at the man who had abandoned him to these streets. He was drenched in sweat and nearly doubled over from the exertion of keeping up with his son, but somehow he had been able to follow.

"I was too late," Trent said. "I don't know if she escaped, and even if she did, who's to say she wasn't killed in another part of the city?"

"Who?"

Anger welled up inside him again at the instant. He turned and lifted the vile man who was his father in name only by the throat. Trent could have snatched the life out of him without any effort. It would have been so easy to give Brandon what he deserved for abandoning his boys to die in these slums.

"My mother," Trent hissed.

Underneath the fear Trent could see a look of confusion play out on his father's face. Trent's anger subsided and he dropped the man.

"Elise," Trent said, turning back to the rubble. "The woman who took Terric and I in. She raised us when you would not. She was a good woman, and I abandoned her."

"High God watch over her," was all his father could mutter.

"We must find the Herald now," Trent said. "If we can cut the head off of the snake, the siege will be more easily pushed back."

"Seraph," a voice hissed.

The hair on the back of Trent's neck stood on end. He spun to see the nearly naked form of the Herald. It was blood-red and covered in rippling muscles. A bushy black beard extended down to its chest. It held a large weapon that almost looked like an over-sized cleaver. Trent eyed the thing, but neither moved.

"You stopped following me, so I had to turn back and see what was so important to you," it said. "And here I find you, crying over some dead woman. At least the last Seraph I killed was strong."

Trent went cold.

Ren.

"The last Seraph?" he asked. His tongue began to stick to the roof of his mouth.

"Yes," the Herald said, stepping forward. "And that was when I was only a Demon. Think of how easily I can kill you now."

Trent froze for a moment, his mind racing. Then he knew the truth. This new Herald was the Demon he had spent his adult life searching for. This Demon was the one who had assassinated Jerrok all those years ago. This Demon was the one who had killed his brother Terric just a few snow-covered streets from here.

The anger returned, but he kept it in check this time even as the smell of his brother's blood returned to his nostrils. He drew Godtaker and pointed it at the Herald.

"I am called Trent," he said, his voice ice. "When you came to this city twenty years ago you didn't just kill the Seraph, you killed a little boy in these very streets. That was my brother Terric. I have waited my entire life to find you. The Fallen One himself could not protect you from me."

Off to the side, Brandon let out an exclamation of shock. He drew his own sword, little good that it would do.

"Y-you killed my son!" he stammered.

The Herald laughed. "I am glad that we are reunited then, Trent the Seraph. I am called Xyx, and I will extinguish your entire family today."

The Herald flew straight at Trent with a snarl. The Seraph batted his enemy away with a blast of lightning and a swing of

Godtaker. Then Xyx was upon him again, the Herald's large weapon cleaving through the air like the work of a butcher at the block. Trent parried each blow that came in rapid succession, his enemy attacking with far more speed and dexterity than his bulky form should have allowed.

"How does it feel to be toyed with, Seraph?" Xyx cooed. "How does it feel to be battered around like a little boy again?"

Trent snarled and threw the Herald back, lancing more fire down the edge of his blade. He knew that Xyx was baiting him. He knew that the Herald was trying to make him lose control. Yet in that moment, he didn't care. He thought of little besides the smell of his brother's blood upon the snow.

Brandon foolishly came up from the rear swinging his own sword wildly. A sharp kick from the taloned feet of the Herald sent the man flying backward with a trail of fresh blood following in his wake. He hit the ground and groaned but did not rise.

Trent hacked into his enemy again and again, cutting at the empty air where the fiend had been standing; nearly always a moment too slow. Just then Xyx took to the air, and Trent followed, a roar erupting from his lips.

"This blade belonged to Arra!" he shouted. "It has killed Divine Beasts and gods alike! And it will return you to the blackness from which you crawled!"

Xyx looked back at the Seraph, a smile crossing his wicked face. Then he dropped his weapon and dove straight into Trent, clawed arms wrapping the Seraph so that Godtaker couldn't be brought to bear. With alarming speed, the two winged figures punched through the roof of a house and into the floor below. An explosion of wood shards and dust filled the small space, blinding Trent. He could feel that one of his wings had been broken again, but otherwise, he was unharmed. He shook his head to clear the spots from his vision, but the Herald was gone.

Suddenly the house erupted into flames. Xyx was madly cackling from outside as black and red flames bathed the structure. What wood didn't instantly turn to ash crackled and splintered as the house collapsed onto Trent in a suffocating, burning heap.

Forgive me Terric.

A flash of fear replaced his rage as Trent struggled to free himself from the inferno. He had allowed his anger to blind him. He had allowed the Herald to trick him, and this was the price. He would never be able to avenge his brother. Never be able to help Ren. He would die here with Elise. With his father.

Clarity struck Trent's mind. He took a deep breath and shoved a burning timber from the top of him. Already his healing magic was rushing to the bones in his wing and the burns on his flesh. The Seraph knew that he could still do this. His father lay out there, wounded, and for some reason that gave him the strength to fight on. It meant that he was something that the Herald was not: human.

As the last of the burning house collapsed Trent flew straight up through the stinging smoke and landed directly in front of his adversary. The Herald flashed another quick smile before stepping back into a more defensive stance. It's weapon had returned to it, and already Xyx look poised to strike once again.

The ash fell heavy on the street between them, coating it like a fine layer of grey snow. They stood across from each other like they had some twenty years past as a little boy and Demon. Brandon limped over to stand beside his son, his face a mask of pain, but his eyes were determined and burned like coals. While he had once been a coward, he now stood tall as he faced his son's killer. Trent felt a pang of longing for what could have been, but quickly pushed it aside.

"Stay out of the way, father," he whispered. Though his words had been harsh, there was no malice in them.

"Never again, son," Brandon replied.

The Herald and Seraph slammed into each other in a shower of blows. Where Trent had once been wild an attacking without thought, he now focused his strikes for any perceived weakness that he saw in the Herald. His father made his way to the creature's flank, hacking wildly at its wings. For a time, Xyx held them both at bay, but then Trent saw the opening he was looking for, and a deft stroke of Godtaker sent the Herald's weapon flying down the street.

Xyx deftly leaped backward, holding his gleaming claws out like they were themselves blades. He cackled then, pressing his hands together in mock prayer.

"Tell me Seraph," he crooned, "do you pray? What little good it does, do you clasp your hands thusly and beseech the Gods of Light to save you?"

Trent and Brandon slowly circled the beast, their eyes stony and their lips silent. Trent was done being baited by this *thing*. In the distance, there was loud rumbling and a cloud of silt and dust rose up on the horizon that seemed to cover half the city. Trent paid it no heed.

"What a pity that prayer seems to be such a wasted effort," the Herald hissed. "Good thing that there are other, more practical uses for hands such as these."

In a flash of red Xyx was on top of Trent, clawing wildly. Each blow from Godtaker was turned aside by the claws that sliced and raked at every piece of exposed flesh the Seraph had. It seemed that even without a weapon, they were evenly matched, until Xyx suddenly sprang backward again, landing just behind the startled Brandon. A thick-fingered hand clutched the man by the throat, drawing five rivulets of blood.

"What now Trent of the slums?" Xyx asked. His smile was wicked. "Once again you get to watch one of your family die by my hand. How does that make you—"

Xyx's diatribe was cut short by a gurgle from his surprised throat. Brandon stood, shuddering, his hands white as he gripped his sword. It was plunged through his stomach at such an angle that it had pierced the Herald through the chest, near to his heart. Shocked, Xyx dropped Brandon who fell to his knees, his sword sliding free from his enemy.

Trent was there in a flash, swinging Godtaker in a savage arc. He nearly removed the head from his foe, but the still-shocked Herald held onto the blade with his blood-stained claws. Trent let go of his sword and gripped the Herald by the horns, ripping his head from his shoulders with a sickening tear. The headless corpse of Terric's killer flopped down into the ash. Trent tossed the head away and rushed to his father.

Brandon was nearly gone already, his eyes fluttering weakly. A bloody smile crossed his face.

"Never again," was all he had the strength to say.

Trent pulled his father's sword free and placed his already glowing hands upon him. This was foolish, given the grievous nature of the wounds his father had suffered. If he could be saved, it would only be at a great loss to Trent's own strength. Still, he kept on.

"Don't," his father hissed, strength returning to his face. "I don't deserve this. Let me die."

"No," Trent whispered. "I'm not saving you for myself, but for Terric. Death is too easy for you, father. You don't get to kill yourself to save your last son and think that somehow absolves you. No. I am saving you because you have a lifetime of penance and guilt to suffer through. That is what Terric is owed."

His father closed his eyes and let out a long sigh. When he was done, Trent cradled the man in his arms and took to the sky, making his way toward the inner city. Brandon's breaths were shallow, but for now, at least, he would live.

Ahead, the path to the inner city was chaos. Divine Beasts rolled in the streets, toppling buildings and sending up clouds of debris in their wake. Of Gil and the people of Seatown, there was no sign. Trent noticed that a crude wall separated the border of the inner city from the rest of Illux and he cursed under his breath. Then he saw the giant chasm where several blocks of the city on both sides of the wall had collapsed.

There was nothing Trent could do but make for the Grand Cathedral.

20

eo.

The voice cut through his mind like a knife. It seemed as if it had been weeks since he had heard it last. The voice that was of himself, but not himself. The voice that he had once thought had been the Grey God speaking to him from beyond death. The voice that he had learned was actually the High God, setting creation back onto the right path.

Teo. Your God has need of you.

Teo ducked under the swinging metallic arm and sprang onto the back of his attacker. These Tempest Born were mindless killing machines, somehow even more dangerous than a Demon. If he allowed it to get ahold of him he would be crushed in an instant. His blows did little to harm the thing, and he felt his strength failing as his battered fists continued to strike the unblemished metal.

You are needed elsewhere Balance Monk.

The voice was clear and drowned out all of the sounds of dying around him. Rella was nearby, fairing a little better than he was. Behind them, Ren was destroying as many of the metallic warriors as she could, while the Demigods harried their flanks. Even without the voice, he knew it was right. What hope did either Balance Monk have against these things? Still, he was loath to leave Rella, even at the behest of the High God.

Teo. You must leave this battle. There is one in need of your salvation. A lost soul who you alone can pull from the flames of hate.

He felt his calm demeanor crack for a moment as he looked at Rella. She was being pushed back by another Tempest Born. He ducked another blow and rolled toward her. Springing from the ground, the Balance Monk slammed into the chest of the Tempest Born with both feet, staggering it back from Rella. She deftly kicked a fallen sword into the air and Teo caught it, shoving the blade into the eye socket of the skeletal beast with all of his might. It shuddered and fell still.

He stumbled backward from the creature and Rella caught him in her arms. The smell of her body, caked in blood and sweat as it was, still filled him with longing. In another life perhaps…

"We must fall back," he said to her. "These creatures are too much for us without the strength of Ravim to call upon."

She nodded as the Tempest Born that Teo had been grappling with slowly walked toward them.

"What shall we do?" she hissed, pulling his arm over her shoulders.

"You should focus on the mortal servants of the fallen Seraph. I am called elsewhere."

Her eyes locked with his but she didn't question him. When they were a safe distance behind the line of Demigods, Rella released Teo. He smiled at her for only a moment before sprinting off into the sprawl of the inner city behind them.

The maze of streets and towering family mansions was dizzying to him without a guide. He had rarely been to Illux during his old life as a bandit, and then it had only been to the slums to sell stolen goods. Somewhere nearby was this lost soul, but where? He hoped that the voice of the High God would come to him again and point the way, but the deity remained silent.

Then he saw the smoke. The entire city burned in one way or another, but this was inside the inner city, and much closer to Teo. Something told him that he could go that way and he would discover that which he was tasked with finding.

After a few long minutes of running, Teo found himself in front of a great mansion, engulfed in flames. None of the surrounding homes burned and the street was empty of any signs of struggle. Something ominous had happened here, and this was where he was meant to go, he knew it.

The Balance Monk took a moment to calm himself before hurrying into the open front door and the roaring flames beyond. Inside the mansion was blisteringly hot, and Teo had to duck beneath the billowing smoke that clung to the ceiling, searching desperately for a way out. While he couldn't recognize any of the family heraldry through the smoke and flames, he could tell that this was a very old and powerful family. No doubt they had been loyal to Castille.

So why ask me to come here?

Teo jumped over a flaming timber and into what had surely been the great hall once. He squinted against the smoke, searching for any sign of life. Then he saw the rough outline of an armored figure kneeling in the middle of the flames. His once-white armor was stained with blood and soot. Teo quietly gasped as he recognized the man as Arkos.

The Balance Monk approached the Paladin with an outstretched hand.

"Arkos," he called. "Arkos, leave this place."

"Devin?" the man replied, his voice hoarse from smoke.

"Come, Lighthammer," Teo pleaded. "There is nothing for you here."

Arkos took the Balance Monk's hand and stumbled to his feet, clutching a great hammer at his side. Together the pair numbly walked out of the carnage of the Lighthammer mansion as its supports finally gave way. Once the rays of the sun greeted them, the building collapsed in on itself, covering the two with dust and smoke.

"What happened?" Teo choked out.

"I found my father," Arkos sighed. "He was an evil man, monk. I did to him what I have done to countless other evil souls in this city over the years. I killed him."

Teo nodded in grim understanding.

"Then why did you stay in the flames?"

"I wished to pay for my own crimes. I am a murderer, nothing more. I have forsaken the light of my cousin for the darkness of my father and called it justice. That is not the way of a Paladin."

"Perhaps not," Teo said evenly, "but your work is not done. We still have a war to win and people to protect. Is that not the work of a Paladin?"

Arkos nodded dumbly, his bluster and arrogance gone.

"Come with me then, and forget your sins. Some day there may come a time for absolution, and perhaps you will help us restart the Grey Temple, or perhaps there will be a need for Paladins who know how easily they can fall into darkness. Either way, the High God has need of you. Come."

Teo stood and headed back to the plaza of the Grand Cathedral. Arkos followed and didn't look back.

21

The Paladin went flying into the gathered Tempest Born, his back loudly cracking against their immovable forms. Ren grimaced. Even in her rage, she felt some pity for these traitors. They were only doing what they thought was right. After all, hadn't she done the same when she had tried to kill Jerrok all those years ago?

Most of the Paladins were cowering inside the Grand Cathedral, leaving the fighting to the Tempest Born. Some, however, like the man she had just killed, had been shut outside and still they fought to protect Castille. Edmund had shattered one of the doors, but the Paladins wasted no time reinforcing it with overturned pews and other debris. Ren knew most of them to be from inner city families that no doubt were raised to believe themselves better than the people of the slums or the villages. Even though she had no intention of ruling Illux when this was over, she knew that the divide between the two halves of Illux would need to be mended once and for all.

Tess and her Demigods were holding their own against the Tempest Born, but Ren knew that it wouldn't last. She needed to get into the Fourth Spire and kill Castille before they were forced to retreat.

Retreat where? The slums aren't safe either.

The Seraph took to the air, flying just out of reach of the metallic warriors below. She made her way directly toward the balcony of the Fourth Spire, the place where Seraphs could come and go as they pleased. She hoped that she would be able to break in more easily there, and then it was just up to her to contend with whatever Castille had on the inside.

Just as she expected, the white door on the balcony was barred shut from the inside. It would take quite some effort to get through—it had been designed to withstand a Herald, after all. Flying back a safe distance Ren pointed Nightbreaker straight at the door as the energy of her blood crackled in the air around her.

"Castille!" she shouted. "Come forth, traitor! Come forth and answer for your crimes against the people of this city!"

There was no response.

Ren let the energy she was channeling go. Lightning hammered into the door with such a thunderous crack that those fighting on the ground looked up. She prepared to strike again when shouts of alarm from below caught her attention. She turned to see a winged shape heading her way from the slums. She couldn't see the face clearly, but it was a Seraph, not a Herald. The other Seraph was also carrying someone in their arms.

Castille! He was somewhere else the entire time.

She cursed at her stupidity for allowing so many lives to be lost while Castille wasn't even in the Grand Cathedral. Ren began winging her way toward her quarry, energy gathering around her once more. It was finally time to finish this. It seemed that Tess and her troops thought the same thing, as blasts of ice and rock tried to knock the Seraph from the air.

Ren was getting closer, her rage building. This was the man who had tried to have her executed. The man who had undermined her for two decades. The man who had abandoned the people of this city. Neither god nor mortal would stop her from ending his life. She raised Nightbreaker, preparing to sear him with holy flame.

"Ren!" a familiar voice shouted.

She nearly dropped her weapon in shock.

It can't be!

"Trent," she whispered, tears flowing freely.

Indeed now she could see the man she loved was the one flying toward her. His face was scarred and he looked more haggard than she remembered, but he was somehow alive. In his arms, he carried an older man who resembled him. Somehow she knew this to be his father. Ren pointed to a spot on the ground behind the bulk of the fighting. Trent nodded and followed her down.

Once they had landed and Trent had released his father they embraced. At first, neither spoke, and both cried openly.

"I thought you were dead," she said finally.

"I nearly was," Trent replied. "I blasted my way out of that creature and then when I awoke I found that my...father, of all people, had pulled me to safety and nursed my wounds for several days."

"Castille is a Seraph now. Luna has made her betrayal of the Light absolute."

"Let us finish this then," Trent said, smiling. "Together."

Just then a cacophony of shouts rose over the din of the fighting. Both Seraphs turned to see the doors to the Grand Cathedral bursting open as hundreds of people flooded out. Ren couldn't make out any faces from this distance, but she recognized the sea-colored cloak of one of the front figures.

"Seatown! But how?" She shouted.

"Gil found a way," Trent said.

The newfound army surged into the plaza, forcing the Tempest Born to defend their flanks as well. Ren knew that even with their superior numbers, thousands would die if she didn't find a way to stop the fighting.

"We have to get to Castille," she said. "Gods be good the Tempest Born will stop fighting us if their Seraph dies."

They have to.

Trent nodded and they both took to the air heading back toward the Grand Cathedral. Even with the lower doors open now, Ren didn't want to risk fighting Castille in an enclosed space, so she angled back for the balcony atop the Fourth Spire. With her and Trent's powers combined they would be able to make it inside much faster. She just hoped that it would be fast enough.

When they were level with the door she nodded at Trent. In moments both Seraphs were bathing the barrier with lightning and flame. The door began to blacken and buckle. Trent waved for Ren to stop. He flew into the door at full speed with his Godtaker held aloft like a battering ram. The door exploded inward and skittered across the floor.

Ren landed inside her old chambers just behind Trent, her face already a snarl. Castille stood opposite them, a small honor guard of Paladins and Tempest Born surrounding him.

"You fucking coward," Ren sneered.

"Traitorous bitch," Castille spat back. "Kill her."

The guards charged the invading Seraphs. Paladins shouted oaths to Luna and Castille while the Tempest Born marched forward in terrifying silence.

"Kill the old man," Trent shouted over his shoulder. "I'll handle this chaff."

Ren knew that the Tempest Born would prove for more trouble than Trent realized, but she also knew that he was right. Castille needed to die, and he needed to die quickly.

Quickly, Ren side-stepped the closest Paladin, severing his head with Nightbreaker. Blood fountained all over her once immaculate chambers. Castille had his own weapon drawn, but he backed away clutching it weakly before him. Even with Divine Blood pumping through his veins, he feared her.

Good.

Nightbreaker sang as it cut through the air. Castille barely deflected the blow. For a moment fear flashed across his face. Then his arrogance returned and he pressed the attack. Masonry exploded around them from the blasts of energy created by Trent and the Paladins. Ren ignored it and kept on. Castille needed to be her focus. He needed to die.

"You were never worthy of this office," he panted. "Arra chose a fool! A traitor! A weakling!"

"I never claimed that I was worthy!" Ren shouted. "Only that I was more worthy than you!"

She lunged, knocking his sword from his hand. Nightbreaker hacked at the base of one of his wings, spraying the tapestry behind them with silver and red.

Castille howled in pain as he blasted Ren backward with lightning. She was caught off guard and slammed into a Tempest Born. The metallic warrior grabbed her by the throat, trying to crush her windpipe. A howl filled the room and Trent severed the silver arms from the creature with one stroke of Godtaker.

She spun to see Castille fleeing out the open door to the balcony. Even as she gasped to return the air to her lungs she raced after him. The plaza below them was filled with thousands of bodies. It seemed that more than just the people of Seatown had used the catacombs to get into the Grand Cathedral. Overwhelmed as they were, bodies piled around the Tempest Born by the dozens.

Castille was heading higher into the air above the cathedral, the wound on his wing nearly closed. Ren quickly closed the gap between them, her throat still burning from the grip of the Tempest Born. As she got closer, she could hear the old man praying under his breath.

"Luna, Goddess of Light, please protect your servant. Luna, Goddess of Light, deliver me. Luna, Goddess of Light, bring me to the Divine Plane. This city is lost."

Ren grabbed him by the foot and yanked him down. He went spinning away from her, tumbling toward the sharp points of the spires below. Her enemy caught himself and flew back at her snarling again, but she knew that his rage was simply masking fear.

She met him head-on, swords clashing in a flurry of silver and black. Lightning crackled around each Seraph, arcing this way and that, slamming into the other or bouncing off of defensive magic back into the spires of the Grand Cathedral. Ren heard a deafening crack and saw that the tip of one of the spires had broken and was falling into the mass of people below.

Cursing, she slammed into Castille with renewed vigor, aiming her attack at his wings once more. She could feel that she was tiring and she would need to end this quickly or she risked being overpowered. Nightbreaker flashed again and again but still, the other Seraph was able to parry her strikes. Ren wouldn't be able to overpower him now; she was losing speed too quickly.

Then she knew what to do. Nightbreaker flew up in the air as Ren threw it overhead. Using both hands, she caught Castille by the wrists, preventing his next swing. She twisted his arms and slammed her forehead into the bridge of his nose. As he cried out his grip on his sword loosened and Ren tossed it away. Nightbreaker began its descent and she caught the blade with her right hand.

Once, then twice she hacked at the base of his right wing. Bone and sinew gave way in a burst of blood and feathers. Castille again cried out in pain, and again Ren hacked at the base of his left wing. When she was done, the grizzled warrior hung limp in her grasp, rivers of crimson and silver raining below.

Ren sheathed Nightbreaker and grabbed Castille by the head

with both hands. Shock and fear washed across his face so thoroughly that she nearly felt pity for him. His healing magic was attempting to close the wounds on his back, but he wouldn't be able to regain his wings, and he knew it.

"Castille Denost," she growled. "You have taken up arms against the rightful Seraph of Illux, and worse, you have betrayed the people of this city and left them to die."

She placed her thumbs into his eye sockets and squeezed. He screamed as the blood rushed over her hands.

"Just as you left the people of Illux to fall into the Darkness, so I leave you."

Ren let go and the man who would have replaced her fell to the plaza below, his screams receding into the distance. The Seraph flew back down to the balcony, Nightbreaker once again in her hands. When she landed she saw Trent covered in blood but alive and panting in the middle of the room, a pile of corpses surrounding him.

"It's done," she said.

"Good," Trent said huskily. "I got him, Ren. The Demon who killed Terric. He had become the Herald. My father and I killed him in the slums."

He smiled weakly at her. She felt a warmth in that smile, but she could see the pain behind it. Killing that Herald had finally brought Trent some measure of peace, but it wasn't all that he had hoped for. Looking down at the gore that streaked her hands, she knew how he felt.

"We have to get below," she said at last. "The Tempest Born must be stopped."

They both returned to the ground to find that the metallic warriors had already stopped fighting. Each now stood inert. Ren landed among them, prodding a few with Nightbreaker. None moved.

"He's dead then?" a deep voice asked.

Ren turned to see Arkos and Teo standing behind her. If either of the newcomers saw Trent, they gave no sign. She smiled in spite of herself. The Paladin must have accomplished whatever he had set out to do.

"He is," she replied.

"You are once again the Seraph of Illux," Arkos said. "Command them."

"Tempest Born!" Ren shouted.

Hundreds of silver heads snapped to attention.

"Open every gate to the inner city. Find every mortal that still lives and keep them safe. Wipe the stain of darkness from Illux once and for all!"

The silver warriors began marching without pause. The city was hers again, and it was time to defend it.

22

"This way!" Rella shouted, pointing at a group of Demons and Accursed that had cornered survivors in the slums. Teo nodded and motioned for the Tempest Born behind him to follow. The steel warriors gave no indication that they understood other than their change in direction. They marched ahead of the Balance Monks, making quick work of the enemy.

So it had gone for hours. The Balance Monks were searching the slums for survivors while the Tempest Born cleaned up pockets of resistance. With the Herald dead and both Seraphs returned, the Forces of Darkness had shattered. The ground still shook from the rumblings of battling Divine Beasts, but the invasion had mostly been repelled.

Somehow we have done it. We have nearly restored the Balance.

Not yet Teo. Have you forgotten me?

The voice that cut through his mind this time gave him pause. It wasn't the voice that he had come to recognize as the High God. It was a voice that he hadn't heard since before he was even a

Balance Monk. A woman he had loved. A woman he had killed. Jyn.

Startled, the Balance Monk looked around the smoky wreckage. There was no one besides Rella, the Tempest Born, and the survivors. He shook his head and continued forward. He was simply too tired and had been hearing voices too long.

"Make for the inner city. The Seraphs and Paladins are there providing healing and distributing provisions," he heard Rella say.

The scared people nodded and ran past, casting a wary glance at the Tempest Born. Teo couldn't blame them. Even he wasn't entirely sure that they could be trusted now. They had been creatures of Luna, after all. Still, he couldn't help but wonder at the providence of their existence now. Without them, he wasn't sure that the exhausted defenders would have been able to finish repelling the invaders.

Ahead, a goat-like beast sprang from the shadows at Rella. She twisted beneath it and threw the creature into the side of a sagging building. It was quickly covered in debris. These sintaurs as they had been named by the Demigods had broken from the second army of Demons and Accursed and now prowled the streets looking for easy meat.

Two Goddesses have come to Mortal Realms and left two new species behind.

He shuddered in spite of himself. The world he had known would never be the same. Aenna above was nearly invisible, the City of Light was a battleground, the Grey Temple a smoldering ruin. And there was no longer a Grey God. Perhaps it was the amount of time they had spent with the Seraphs, but Teo was beginning to feel the walls of his resolve crumbling. He was finding himself wondering if he would be better off as a Paladin. Broderick Breaksword had once done such a thing…

"Teo."

This time he was sure that the voice of Jyn hadn't been in his mind. He searched again for its source but saw nothing. Rella hadn't reacted, so perhaps he was still imagining things. Teo swallowed hard but pressed on. They would be done soon, and could finally rest.

More Demons sprang from the shadows ahead, dispatching one of the Tempest Born. Teo and Rella ran to assist their metal troops but it didn't matter, they had already made quick work of the Demons before the Monks even arrived. Perhaps they weren't needed and they could return to the inner city. He glanced again at Rella; her face was a mask of grim determination. She wasn't going to rest until this was truly done.

A movement out of the corner of Teo's eye caught his attention. He spun, his staff raised defensively. Through the swirls of smoke, he saw a familiar face. Then she was gone.

Jyn.

Ignoring Rella's calls he sprinted into the malaise after the woman that he knew to be dead.

RELLA EITHER WOULD NOT or had not been able to follow him. He supposed that he was thankful for that even though he felt a pang of regret. Still, he knew that something was going on that was meant for him alone. Why else would he be seeing this specter?

"Who are you?" he shouted ahead at the dark shape that was running from him.

Have you forgotten me?

She was in his head again, but this time he knew it wasn't exhaustion. This was something else. Memories of Jyn flooded his mind, nearly causing him to stop running. They had fought together as bandits. He had loved her then, as much as a man like that was capable of love. Then she had betrayed him and he had been forced to kill her. That's what he had told himself, in any case. It wasn't long after she had died that Teo had found himself at the Grey Temple and given himself over to Ravim.

So why was she here, now?

The Balance Monk rounded another corner and found himself staring directly into Jyn's eyes. He shuddered and stumbled backward, dropping his staff and falling to the ground. She leaned over him, her body unclothed just as she had been when he had killed her.

"You didn't forget me, did you Teo?" she asked.

"N-no," he stammered. "I could never forget you. Why are you here?"

"You killed me," she said softly. "Don't you remember?"

Suddenly Teo was on top of her again, his hands around her throat. He tried to pull them free but she held him fast. Already her face was beginning to turn blue. He heard the sickening snap of her arm from the weight of his knee. Her knife clattered harmlessly to the cobblestones.

"You didn't have to do it," she whispered. "You had a choice."

"You were going to sell me to the Paladins!" he shouted, anger filling his voice.

He squeezed tighter, his guilt and anger mingling into one nebulous emotion.

"You had a choice, Teo," she whispered. "You chose violence. That is what you have always chosen. You said you loved me and yet you killed me."

"There was nothing I could do!"

His tears splattered her face.

"I'm sorry! You're right! I'm sorry!"

"You found peace at the Grey Temple, but you never truly forgave yourself. You gave your life to Balance, but you never gave your soul."

"What do you want from me?" Teo asked, his voice shaking.

"Everything."

Her face was dark purple now. She placed her fallen knife into his hands. The Balance Monk sat back on his heels, his stomach churning.

"I did betray you, Teo," she said. "I would have killed you. You were a murderer, but so was I. You turned from the path of Darkness. You must do so one more time, to truly restore the Balance."

"I don't understand."

She sat up, color returning to her face. Jyn's fingers wrapped around his hands and she pulled the knife closer until its point was in her breast.

"You must kill me again Teo. Face your sins. You will know what to do afterward."

"No!" he shouted, recoiling. "I can't! Not again!"

"Light versus Darkness. The cycle will continue unless you do this!"

"Why me?"

"Because you have been a good man and an evil one in equal measure. Only you can do what needs to be done."

He swallowed and looked down at his shaking hands. The grey tattoos seemed to swirl before his eyes.

"Forgive me," he said.

The knife sank deep into her chest. She shuddered but didn't cry out. The blood that ran down her breast was silver, not red. Teo stared at the wound in shock. Then Jyn pulled free the knife and stabbed Teo in the heart. He collapsed beside her, his vision fading as his blood left his body.

Then he felt it. Everything at once.

23

They had truly done it.

Illux was saved, at least for the moment. In the next few hours the Forces of Darkness would be fully routed. With their Herald dead and their numbers depleted from the skirmishes with the other armies outside the walls, the broken force that now occupied Illux was being swept away by the Tempest Born with little resistance.

Trent looked over the scarred plaza around the Grand Cathedral. The inner city was a ruin, but it was also full of survivors. The people gathered here were getting medical aid from the Paladins who had stayed loyal to Ren. Defenses were being prepared in case Luna or the Fallen One had any further tricks, but Trent didn't feel that it would be necessary. The enemy had been defeated, and they had bought the people of the Mortal Plane time to rebuild.

How long though?

The Seraph could see the shapes of the Divine Beasts circling the perimeter of the city. They had slaughtered the dark god's monsters and now simply helped root out the last pockets of

187

Demons that hid in the slums. Somehow they had done so without suffering any further deaths beyond Aion.

The thought gave Trent pause. He took to the air and scanned the milling bodies below for a sign of his dearest friend. Though he didn't see Gil, he did find the blue-green cloak of Admiral Wyn Thacker. The Seraph quickly winged his way down toward her, landing among a group of Seatown citizens who seemed to be deep in argument.

"We should leave by the evening!" one shouted at the Admiral. "We have fulfilled your oath to the Lady Ren. It's time to find the rest of our people!"

"The sea is safe again. We have the chance to find new lands!" shouted another.

"No!" A woman exclaimed. "It isn't safe yet. There could be hundreds of Demons between here and the coast. The Nameless Sea will wait. We cannot abandon the people here."

Wyn looked at each in turn but said nothing. This was the first time Trent had seen her at a loss for words. Then she looked at Trent and her expression softened.

"The war isn't over," Wyn said, holding up her hands to silence the others. "I take the Lady Ren as a woman of her word, and we will go when we are released from our charge."

She nodded at her companions and walked over to Trent. The group left with several murmurs of dissent but they knew better than to continue the debate in front of one of the Seraphs. As she got closer Trent thought that he could see the glimmer of tears in her eyes.

"Where is Gil?" Trent asked.

"He led us through the Catacombs, but he had pushed himself too far. He stayed behind to collapse the tunnel on the enemies that followed us."

Trent looked away from her then, his first bawled up so tightly he felt his gauntlets straining. Deep down he had known as soon as the people of Seatown had emerged from the cathedral and he had not seen Gil.

"He died a good man, my lord," she whispered. "He saved thousands. Possibly this whole city. If the Demons had made it through the tunnels into the inner city…"

She trailed off, unable to meet Trent's gaze when he finally looked back at her.

"Gil felt tremendous guilt over whatever happened in Seatown before Ren and I got there. He felt like he failed us, Devin and I. What he didn't realize was that he was always the best of us. I fought the Forces of Darkness for revenge, Devin for glory, but Gil? He fought to protect people. That's why he stayed in Rinwaithe, then Marna. That's why he did whatever he did in Seatown."

"I know. When the fighting is over, I ask that we can recover his body and give him a burial in the sea among my people."

Trent wished that he could have buried Gil here in Illux beside Devin, but he knew that they would likely never find Devin's body. He sighed and nodded his head.

"Yes, but I wish to find his body now. When you return home, let him rest with your heroes."

Wyn flashed a faint smile as Trent took to the air. He made his way toward the section of the city that had collapsed into the catacombs.

When he landed, faint swirls of dust still spun in the air. He surveyed the wreckage and knew that he was undertaking an impossible task. The tunnel that Gil had brought down had started a chain reaction that had taken out several blocks in every direction. It would take weeks to clear. Still, he felt like he at least had to try.

Scanning the large pit, Trent focused on where he thought the center had been and began to toss rubble aside. It wasn't long before he found the first bodies. Dozens of black-armored brutes had been crushed here, along with the pulverized corpses of Accursed. Each that Trent found was cast aside like the detritus they were and he moved on.

After what felt like hours, he collapsed, laying back against the remains of a pillar. Tears began to flow like a torrent. Not just for Gil, but Devin, Elise, and Terric as well. All lost to the machinations of a fallen god. Trent pulled his knees close to his chest and let the sobbing wrack his body. He was a little boy again, falling in the scarlet snow beside the body of his brother. He hadn't been able to save any of them. He had killed Akklor the Unbidden, and he had killed the Herald Xyx, but still his friends and family were dead, and he was alive for some reason.

The High God had tried to tell him that Terric would have made that same choice again, but in that moment Trent wished that he hadn't. He wished that he had died so that all of the pain and suffering he had experienced had never happened.

No. There was good too.

His thoughts shook free of the grief. He needed to continue to live, for them.

And there is still one who needs to face justice for their deaths. Lio. I don't know how, but I am coming for you.

The sound of wings broke him from his thoughts of vengeance. He looked up to see Ren descending to land beside him. He smiled and wiped away the tears as he rose to meet her. She embraced him but said nothing, gently running her fingers through his hair.

"Lio and Luna will pay for this," she said. "I swear it to you, my love. This isn't over until the Mortal Plane is free of their taint. I will make that coward Samson bring us to the Divine Plane and you and I will kill the gods."

His sadness didn't fade, but it was matched by something warmer. Out of the corner of his eye, Trent saw the glint of something white. He turned from Ren and crouched down to remove the rubble from that area. His fingers brushed against the armor, and Trent knew that he had found him.

"It's him," he croaked.

Ren rushed to his side, and together they removed the crushed body of their fallen friend from the rubble. Gil's face had been mostly unharmed, and he looked like he was finally at peace. Trent smiled in spite of himself.

Enjoy your time together, you two. I will be joining you shortly.

The two Seraphs carried the fallen hero back to the plaza of the Grand Cathedral. When they arrived they saw that both Tyr and the Guardian had returned. As they landed, both Divine Beasts bowed in respect for the fallen warrior. Wyn saw them and did the same. In moments the entire plaza had fallen to their knees for the Paladin that had saved them.

Finally, Wyn and several of her people took Gil's body from the Seraphs and carried him back to the tents they had begun setting up in the shadow of the cathedral. Trent said goodbye to his friend and turned back to Ren.

"Contact him. It's time we finish this," he said.

"It is," boomed a voice that boomed like thunder, "but not the way you think."

The Seraphs turned to see Teo standing before them. At least, the figure had once been Teo. Now his entire body was the same color as the grey tattoos that had once covered his skin. If it wasn't for the movement of his mouth, it would almost seem that he was made of stone.

"What?" Ren asked.

"Teo!" Rella called out from the other side of the crowd. "Thank Ravim you are here! When I lost you I came back looking for—"

The Balance Monk's words caught in her throat as she got closer. Suddenly the look of shock on her face became one of reverence as she fell to her knees.

"The Grey God!" she exclaimed.

At that moment Trent realized that Rella was right. Teo was no longer a Balance Monk, but the God of Balance. Instinctively he looked at Aenna and saw that the window to the Divine Plane was indeed brighter than it had been before. Somehow a new god walked among them.

"How?" Trent asked.

"The High God came to me as an old friend. I now know what we must do. Take my hands."

As soon as they did Trent felt them ascending toward Aenna in a blinding flash of light.

24

When the blinding light faded Ren found herself standing on the Divine Plane once again. This time she stood inside a circle of pillars on a floor of smooth stone the same color as Teo's skin. Trent and Rella seemed just as disoriented as she was. Near the edge of the pillars seemed to be a headless corpse that to her eye looked like it could have belonged to the man-turned-god before her.

Ravim. So this is the Grey God's shrine.

"Listen closely," Teo said, his voice much harsher than it had ever been when he had been a mortal. "We do not face simple Demons or Heralds, we face gods. Even the Divine Beasts we have killed will seem as gnats to these. They will move before you can see them, strike before you know they are there. The only chance you have against them is trickery and using weapons forged on this plane."

Ren looked at Godtaker and Trent nodded.

"Do not forget your own blade, Ren," Teo said, following her gaze. "Nightbreaker was originally Lio's sword before he gifted it to Daniel."

"Teo, my-my lord," Rella interjected. "If that is the case, why have you brought me as well?"

A flash of human emotion crossed his face.

"To bear witness," he replied, "and I would not be parted from you again."

Rella seemed to blush as she nodded. Ren still struggled to take it all in. Fear threatened to overtake her, but she brushed it aside. Nothing would prevent her from getting justice for her people. Not even the gods.

"This way," Teo said, walking out of the pillars.

As he passed the headless corpse of his forebear he paused momentarily but said nothing. Rella bowed her head in respect as she did the same. Something about this new Grey God was off to Ren. He seemed even less human than the original gods did. Was that simply a part of his transformation, or did he know something that the wasn't telling his friends? Something that would make him suppress his emotions?

Ahead, the grey stone seemed to stretch on forever. To their right, Ren could see the forests that led to Ayyslid in the distance, and the faint fires of Infernaak to the left. She shuddered in spite of herself due to how exposed they were out here. Luna and the Fallen One could attack them at any time, yet it seemed that Teo walked ahead with little worry.

Is he truly just the Grey God? Or is he something more?

Rising before them was the High God's Throne. The stone chair that looked over all of creation. Seeing it again, even after everything they had been through, made Ren's breath catch in her throat. She had spoken to the being that had once sat here, looking at all that She had made. Ren wished that they had time to stop and enjoy this place, but what was coming next was far more important.

The group rounded the throne and saw two figures standing beside the Basin of Aenna, looking down at the Mortal Plane below. She pulled out Nightbreaker and heard Trent do the same with Godtaker. Teo's earlier warning filled her ears again.

They will move before you see them.

She steeled herself and prepared to advance. The Grey God held up a hand that bid her to wait.

"You have answered my call," he said loudly to the figures ahead.

Then Ren saw who they were. Samson and Rhenaris. A God of Light and a Goddess of Darkness.

"What is this madness?" Rhenaris spat, the spines along her body rising.

"I am the new Grey God," Teo said.

"That's impossible!" shouted Samson, though his eyes fell to Trent and Ren.

"The High God came to me, and charged me with restoring balance to her creation."

Both gods drew their weapons, warily circling the Basin. Ren held no love for Samson any longer, but her pulse quickened at the thought of raising arms against the last true God of Light.

"Will you join us in this charge?" Teo asked. "My mortal companions are sworn to end the scourge of the Fallen One and the traitor Luna. I seek to aid them in that task."

Samson and Rhenaris shared a wary glance but lowered their weapons. So it seemed that Samson trusted his millennium-long enemy more than he trusted his own Seraphs. Ren stifled a laugh.

The world would be better without gods.

She almost regretted the thought. Almost.

"I find it hard to believe that the High God would return," Samson said. "Or that he would gift a mortal with the power of godhood. But what choice do we have? My wounds have been healing slowly, but I am still wary to fight the Fallen One in my current state, let alone a new God of Balance…"

"Why even come here?" Rhenaris asked. "We've seen through

Aenna that Illux is won. Lio and Luna's plans are destroyed. It would take hundreds of years for them to regain what they have lost and attempt to conquer the Mortal Plane again."

Teo stepped closer to the other two gods, his stance firm but his hands raised in a placating gesture.

"The Fallen One has done too much to disrupt the balance of creation. His existence can no longer be allowed. Divine Blood must be spilled on this day."

Samson looked at Rhenaris again, his eyes avoiding Ren's.

"We…have been discussing the terms of a new Pact," he said. "If we could be rid of Luna and the Fallen One, we would rule as one God of Light and One Goddess of Darkness. No more open war. We will simply embody the choice between good and evil for the mortals as He intended."

Teo nodded, but Ren noticed a flicker of something from his human side again. She thought that he looked as he had when he had led them back to the Grey Temple to secretly dispose of Gaxxog the Incorrigible. There was something that he wasn't telling any of them. She looked to Trent and Rella and it seemed that they hadn't noticed. Rella was still lost in wonder at being on the Divine Plane with a restored Grey God, and Trent had the uneasy look of a soldier right before an attack.

Something is wrong.

A hiss of alarm brought her to her senses. She spun to see two more figures behind them. One was the golden-skinned form of Luna, while the other pallid and hunched figure was certainly the Fallen One.

"So the call was from a new god," Luna cooed. "How can this be?"

"You brought them here?!" Rhenaris asked.

"Who are you?" Lio hissed.

"I am the Balance," Teo said coldly. "I am the Grey God."

25

Everything seemed to happen at once.

The Fallen One and Luna drew their weapons and sprang at Rhenaris and Samson with snarls. Samson began loosing arrows at his attackers. Teo shielded Rella from harm. And the two Seraphs stood watching in wide-eyed disbelief.

Trent gripped Godtaker in both hands, holding it in front of himself like it would do any good. When he saw the speed with which the four gods did battle he realized how futile his desire for justice had been. Even with Divine Blood pumping through his body, he was just a mortal, and these were gods.

The Seraph stepped backward as the two sides made contact. Sword met flail and arrows found purchase in gaps of armor. Though they often moved faster than he could see, what flashes of violence did register before his eyes reminded him of the old tales. In this instance, that wasn't comforting.

What can we hope to do?

Ren gripped his arm and pointed at the Basin of Aenna. The fighting was happening on the edge closest to them. If they could

197

circle around perhaps they could find an opening to do something...

Then Teo looked at them, his eyes remorseful for a moment. He raised his hands and Trent felt a strength enter his body that he had never known before. Suddenly the movements of the gods weren't too fast to follow. He wasn't sure what was happening, but somehow he knew that he would be able to match them, at least for a time. Beside him, Ren seemed equally awestruck.

Both Seraphs ran around the Basin of Aenna, the placid silver surface showing the smoking city of Illux below. When they had moved to the other side of the fighting, Trent watched in awe and Luna and Rhenaris fought in a flurry of blows. Each strike from Luna's hammer was turned aside by a swing from one of the dark goddess's flails. Samson was fairing worse, with the Fallen One overwhelming his defenses with savage blows.

Then Teo jumped into the fray, tossing Lio aside and striking Luna's face and chest with open palms. The Goddess stumbled backward a moment before cursing and knocking Teo back again. Suddenly Lio was on the Grey God's back, baring him into the Basin. At the last moment, Teo rolled free, twisting the arm of his assailant and casting his sword away.

Trent and Ren both joined Rhenaris in the attack on Luna. Though she fought hard, the Goddess found it more challenging to parry three blows. Even so, she began to laugh.

"Mortals!" Luna shouted. 'You come at me with mortals?"

The goddess ducked a flail and kicked the feet out from under Ren. Her hammer nearly crushed the Seraph, but Trent was able to parry the blow with Godtaker. The force of the blow from the goddess brought him to his knees. She laughed again before jumping back away from the range of Rhenaris's flails.

"Teo!" Rella yelled.

Trent turned to see the God of Balance thrown back with a bloody wound in his chest. Samson shouted and rushed forward to attack Lio's back. A gauntleted backhand sent him spinning end-over-end and his bow skittering away on the stone.

Rhenaris charged Luna again, her flails spinning wildly. Trent and Ren each stood and circled around to flank the goddess. A flail wrapped around the hammer and Rhenaris tried to yank the weapon loose. She failed spectacularly as Luna swung the hammer, sending the goddess toppling into Ren. The women fell in a jumble at the God of Darkness's feet. Then Luna raised her hammer and brought it down in one fluid motion.

Trent cried out as the Divine Plane around him grew dimmer. Still dripping with silver blood, Luna's hammer raised to strike again. Ren tried to crawl to safety but she was too slow. The first strike had missed her when it had crushed the head of Rhenaris, but this time she wouldn't be able to escape.

An arrow sprouted from Luna's throat. She gurgled in shock and dropped her hammer. As she fell to her knees Ren stood over her.

"You betrayed the mortals you were supposed to protect. You were never worthy of us," she said.

Nightbreaker flashed and the head of Luna fell. Trent turned back to Samson and the god weakly nodded at them.

At the base of the High God's Throne, Teo and the Fallen One jumped around one another, each landing blow after blow that shook the ground around them. The stone chair was crumbling beneath their assault. Trent swallowed hard and stepped toward them. Lio had been the most powerful of the gods before and after his fall. This battle was far from over. He felt fear threaten to crush him again. Somehow, after everything, he was scared again.

For Gil.

He moved in closer.

For Devin.

He reached the base of the throne.

For Terric.

He sprang into the air, his throat raw from the scream that he bellowed.

Teo caught the Fallen One by the wrist and held him fast. Trent flew through the air with Godtaker raised over his head. He would be the one to end this. Over a thousand years of conflict over with one sword stroke.

Then the Fallen One punched Teo in the face with so much force that the Grey God crumpled into a heap on the throne. Lio turned and caught Trent by the arms, holding the winged warrior like a parent holding an unruly child.

"None of you have ever stood a chance."

Trent heard his arms snap before he felt it. His screams blended with those from Ren and Rella. Arrows from Samson punched into the Fallen One but it made no difference. The Seraph was dropped and he fell limply to the base of the throne.

"Trent!" he heard Ren shout.

Then he heard her and Samson both cry out in rapid succession. There was nothing he could do to protect them. They had made it this far just to fail. It had all been for nothing.

Gentle hands lifted his head. He saw Rella leaning over him.

"You must get up," she said. "You cannot let him win, Trent. Teo doesn't stir. Ren and Samson are nearly dead. You must get up."

Trent blinked as he looked at her face. She looked more like his mother now than he remembered. He smiled. Standing behind her was Terric. He was smiling as well.

"Trent!" She gasped. "*He is killing Ren!*"

Reality rushed back to him. He was overwhelmed with pain. His arms were both broken and he felt the extra strength lent to him by Teo fading. He probed his injuries and knew that they were too severe to truly heal. Then he heard Ren screaming in pain again.

"He's toying with her Trent," Rella pleaded. "Get up!"

His healing magic flared to life. He pulled himself to his knees and felt around for Godtaker. His fingers numbly responded to him and he was able to grip the sword, even as silver and red blood made it slick. The Seraph stood with the aid of Rella and stumbled toward the Fallen One.

Samson lay motionless against the Basin, a deep gash on his forehead. Ren dangled from her hair as the Fallen One twisted her wings at odd angles. Trent saw her suffering and felt the pain in his arms fading as his rage took hold. Lio took no notice of the pair that made their way toward his back, but Trent knew that he would have one chance to end this and save the woman he loved.

Not again. No one I love dies again.

Then he knew exactly what he needed to do.

Trent stood straighter, motioning for Rella to fall back. He pushed the last few steps forward and gave up the element of surprise.

"Lio," he said, as confidently as he could. "Lio stop this. Don't you recognize me?"

Ren fell to the ground where she lay moaning in pain. The Fallen One turned and looked at Trent in confusion.

"Lio, my love," Trent said. "It's me, Daniel."

"Daniel?" Lio asked, his eyes distant.

It was the hesitation that Trent needed. He plunged Godtaker into the Fallen One's chest. The one-time God of Light let out a final sigh as the Divine Plane dimmed and he dropped to the ground.

Trent rushed to Ren, holding her in his lap.

"You did it," she said, smiling through the pain. "How?"

"Love," Trent answered, cradling her broken body.

Beside them, Samson stirred. The injured god crawled over to the pair, placing his hands on them. Trent felt the warmth of the healing power of Divine Blood wash over him. Even the tightness from the scarring on his face vanished.

"It's funny," Samson said when he had finished, and both

Seraphs were whole again, "that the High God gave us the ability to heal mortals, but not ourselves."

Trent and Ren helped him to his feet and walked with him back to the High God's Throne. Rella was likewise holding Teo up. All around them the Divine Plane had dimmed so much it seemed a dream. Trent could see through the High God's Throne to the shrine in the distance. There were now only two gods left. It was over.

"What do we do now?" Rella asked.

"We rebuild," Samson said. "We make a better world than the one before."

"That is for them to do," Teo said. "Not us."

Suddenly the Grey God moved as if he was uninjured. His hands grabbed Samson by the head and he twisted. A loud crack signaled further dimming on the plane and the last God of Light fell.

"Why!?" Ren cried out.

Trent raised Godtaker again.

"I was tasked with restoring the Balance," Teo intoned. "I have nearly done so. The Mortal Plane will be better off without gods."

"But we will still have you," Rella observed.

"Not for very long," Teo sighed. "I will return you to Illux, and then I will take my own life. The Divine Plane shall finally fade back into the ether, and mortals can create their own destinies."

"Surely this cannot be what She wants?" Trent asked, lowering his sword. "She did not ask you to do this!"

Teo smiled, his humanity returning.

"She did, friend. From the moment she gave me her blood I knew what I had to do. Now please, step toward the Basin."

"No!" Rella shouted. "Teo, I love you. Don't do this. We were going to restart the order!"

"And you will," Teo said. "I have lived two lives in one body. One evil and one good. It's time now for that body to rest." He looked over his shoulder at something the rest of them couldn't see. "Jyn. It's time then."

The blood of the Basin began to boil and churn as the three companions fell into it. Before they reached Illux Trent knew without looking back that Aenna had finally winked out.

The Tempest Born stood silently, a statue of steel. Edmund stared at the thing with unease, but he knew that it would never move again. As soon as Luna had died all of her metallic creations had stopped moving. Now Illux was littered with statues that were too heavy to easily move. He figured that they would figure out something to do with them eventually.

His broken arm tied up in a sling, the Captain of the City Watch walked the bustling streets of his city alone. He was still trying to take in all that had happened over the last few days. The gods—all of them—were dead. The people of Illux were truly alone. Worse than this, Liara, his closest friend and confidant, the one member of the Watch he trusted above all others, had been killed protecting the gatehouse from the Herald.

Trent, who it turned out was not dead, told Edmund that her final words had been that he was a damned good captain. What did that matter if those who served under him ended up dead? Even so, he knew that she had died for a better Illux, a better world, and he aimed to make that happen. His defense of the city had made people view him as a hero, and though he didn't feel like one, he planned to use that respect to influence the two Seraphs into making sure that the mistakes of the past were not repeated. Illux would no longer be a city cloven in two. The inner city would not exist in contrast to the slums. All would be one.

Too many died because we allowed it to be otherwise.

The corruption in the City Watch ran to the root. They had become nothing but glorified enforcers to the inner city families. Though it pained him, Edmund knew that he would need to disband the organization now that the siege was over. He would figure a better way to protect the people than armed guards.

He pondered this dilemma as he walked back into the plaza in the center of the city. The Paladins wouldn't be much help either. With the death of the last of the Gods of Light, all of them had lost their powers. True, they were still big brutes, but none could heal or summon holy fire any longer. The Divine Blood that they had called upon to do that had never been their own, and now all of it had been spilled.

Ahead, a crowd was gathering at the base of the Grand Cathedral. Bells in the remaining spires rang to let all those in the city know that the lady was preparing to speak. Edmund wasn't sure exactly what she planned to say, but he knew that the people of the city needed to hear what was going to happen next. All could see that Aenna was gone. Already the rumors were spreading that Trent and Ren had slain all of the gods. That news had been met with a mixed response among the populace. Fear threatened to take hold of the city if the Lady Ren didn't put minds at ease soon.

Edmund's mind wandered to the boy Ajax. He wasn't sure what to do with him now. Elise and Trent had been reunited, and the latter's gratitude had been immense. Even so, Edmund could tell that the siege had been hard on the old woman, and he wasn't sure how much time she had left. Once she passed he would once again need to find a home for the orphan.

The captain climbed the steps onto the makeshift platform that sat at the base of the Grand Cathedral. As he was recognized his ears were greeted by a chorus of people chanting his name in the crowd below. He felt his cheeks get hot, but he tried to keep his expression as stoic as he could. The adoration of the people was not for him.

Standing on the platform was a ragged assortment of priests, some Paladins and Demigods, the two Seraphs and their Balance Monk companion, the Admiral from Seatown, and standing apart, Tess and the white tiger called Divinity.

Edmund made his way to Tess and stood beside her looking out at the sea of faces. It was clear that most of the survivors of the Mortal Plane now filled the plaza. They were so few. And now they had no gods to protect them.

"This should be interesting," Tess whispered.

"You think?" Edmund snickered.

"Perhaps they tear us apart for killing the gods?"

"Us? I was unconscious at the time. And where were you?"

Tess let loose a sly smile. "Catching up with an old girlfriend."

"Is it serious?" Edmund asked.

"It is now, yeah," Tess muttered.

The last stragglers seemed to gather at the edges of the crowd. Edmund was taken aback at how many heads he counted with streaks of white in their hair. The Demigods hadn't suffered the losses that he had expected.

High God be praised.

"Your sister?" Edmund asked.

"Safe. Castille never learned it was her feeding us information. Probably the bravest thing she ever did."

The ringing of the bells stopped, and both Seraphs stepped forward. The low din of the crowd faded as the gathered people strained to hear what their leaders were going to say.

"People of Illux, of Seatown, of the Mortal Plane, rejoice, for we have defeated the Gods of Darkness once and for all!" Ren began. Cheers filled the plaza to a deafening level. She raised her hands to quiet them after a moment. "But it was not without great cost. Each of us has lost loved ones, our homes, our feeling of safety. Indeed, we have also lost our gods."

The people began to cry out and the murmurs threatened to prevent any further speaking from Ren. When they finally died down again she continued.

"The rumors are true. The Gods of Light are also dead. Luna betrayed the people of the Mortal Plane and allied herself with the Fallen One. She paid the price for this and died by my hand. Arra died saving Trent and I during the battle of the Great Chasm, and Samson…was finally killed alongside the Fallen One. That leaves us to find our own path, without their guidance.

"For this reason, I am decreeing that the church now only focuses its worship on the High God, our creator who did not abandon us as we had thought. Without her intervention, all may have been lost."

The murmurs began again. Edmund had known about this part of the speech at least, and it was going over about as well as he could have hoped. Telling people that they needed to change their entire religion was no small ask. While the High God had always been worshiped in Illux, it had always been secondary to the other three. And now they were dead.

"Next, I fulfill an oath I made several weeks ago to the people of Seatown," Ren continued. "For their valiant service in the defense of their sister city, I release them from the rule of Illux. Seatown and any who wish to join them, are free to forge their own path, separate from ours."

The Admiral smiled and embraced Ren in a hug that seemed to surprise both of them.

"As for Illux itself," Ren paused here, her face pained. "We shall rebuild this city. No longer will the slums toil in the shadow of the inner city. All will prosper in our new future. The old families have fled, and their crimes will not be forgotten.

"However, Trent and I will not be staying in Illux. We have chosen to relinquish power and go our own way. It is time for the Mortal Plane to be governed by mortals alone."

Gasps and cries rose from the crowd. Shocked people began to wail and scream questions at the Seraphs. Ren looked back at them, stone-faced. Edmund felt his stomach twist into knots. He hadn't expected that at all. Who would take the place of a Seraph?

"My lady?" Tess shouted over the din.

Ren again quieted the crowds.

"May I make a suggestion?" the Demigod asked over the silence. Ren nodded. "This city was saved by a man of the people, and if they would have him, it should be ruled by a man of the people as well. I say if we no longer have Seraphs in the Fourth Spire, then the only man fit to lead us is Edmund, hero of Illux, who above all others kept his oath!"

Edmund nearly fainted. He felt Tess holding him up as the crowd cheered.

"So shall it be then!" Ren boomed. "Edmund Oathkeeper, you shall be called, the first King of Illux."

In that moment Edmund wasn't sure which of the two women he hated more. The cheering of the crowd drowned out all of his thoughts and he grimly nodded at the people.

He had a long road ahead.

27

"So I guess this is goodbye then," his father said.

"Aye," Trent replied.

The pronouncement hung in the air between them. Trent and Ren stood near the northern gate, their horses saddled with enough provisions to last them several weeks in the Rim. Shortly after returning to the Mortal Plane, Ren informed Trent of her decision to step down as the ruler of Illux. He could tell by her expression that she wasn't sure how he would take the news. Truth be told he was relieved, and so they had decided to journey to the Rim and find somewhere quiet to build a home and leave the fate of the world to others.

Ren reached out and patted Brandon on the shoulder.

"Thank you," she said. "For saving what I thought was lost."

"It wasn't enough, my lady," he replied. "A lifetime of it won't be enough."

"But it's a start," Rella interjected as she returned with horses of her own.

The Balance Monk handed one of the reigns to Brandon. He

nodded and mounted the horse, his eyes meeting Trent's one last time.

"We should be off," Rella said, hugging Trent and Ren in turn. "I know the King wished to see you off, so we'll leave you to it. We have a long road ahead of us."

"What will you do if no one else comes back to the Temple?" Trent asked.

Rella smiled and ran her fingers through the stubble of hair that was starting to obscure the tattoos on her head.

"They'll come, Trent, of that I have no doubt. We will find our own path toward Balance now, but the world will always need the Balance Monks."

Gracefully, she hopped onto her own horse and turned it toward the gate. In a few short moments, Rella and Trent's father were leaving Illux and making their way back to the ruins of the Grey Temple, the last Balance Monk and her first initiate.

It was an odd feeling seeing his father ride away for the last time. Trent had spent a lifetime hating the man, and now all he felt was indifference. Yet deep down he knew that the indifference could become forgiveness one day.

Is that what you would have wanted?

The Seraphs turned back to the road leading to the center of the city as the sounds of the royal procession greeted their ears. Edmund rode at the head of a contingent of royal guards which were made up of former members of the City Watch and several Demigods handpicked by Tess. The woman herself rode next to him with Divinity padding beside her; behind them was Arkos Lighthammer and a wagon whose passengers Trent couldn't guess.

Edmund hopped down from his horse and clapped Ren and Trent on the arms in greeting. His eyes beamed but his face was worn from the last days as King. Trent knew that he didn't want the job, which was why he might have been one of the few people fit for it. Tess dismounted as well while Arkos opened the wagon.

"I wish you'd stay," Edmund said.

"The time for Seraphs has passed," Ren said. "The people of Illux need a leader who stood by them through the entire siege. That is you, Edmund. Trent and I need to rest."

"And if we need your help in the future?" Edmund asked.

Tess put a hand on his shoulder.

"You have enough Divine Blood in your kingdom, let them be," Tess said firmly.

Edmund blushed and nodded. Divinity rubbed her head on the legs of both Seraphs before returning to Tess.

"She really took a liking to you," Ren observed.

"I have no idea why," Tess said. "Even so, she's a good companion. I look forward to her help as I hunt Demons these coming weeks."

Trent shot her a look of confusion.

"Someone has to finish cleaning up this mess," Tess explained. "There are still packs of the bastards roaming around the Wilderness, and by my reckoning, two Heralds unaccounted for. I'm not leaving that to chance."

"Your kingdom is in good hands then," Ren said to Edmund.

Arkos stepped up to the group with the shriveled form of Elise clinging to his arm. Trent felt the world fall out from under him. He had told her goodbye in his own way a few days before and selfishly hoped that would be the end of it. He should have known better.

"Take care of my boy," Elise whispered to Ren as she got close.

Ren gently hugged the old woman, tears in her eyes.

"We will take care of each other," she whispered back.

Then his mother was grabbing his face like he was a little boy again, and he knew that he would never truly be anything but. She looked into his eyes and had the biggest smile that Trent had ever seen on her face.

"You did it," she said.

"Did what, mother?" he choked.

"You forgave yourself. I love you, my son."

"I love you too."

They embraced in silence for a long time. The others of the group breaking off to have side conversations so as not to interrupt their parting. When they were done, Tess walked her back to the wagon and helped her back inside.

"She'll live with me for the rest of her days," Edmund said. "I wouldn't let my son live somewhere unguarded, nor would she let someone else raise the boy."

Trent laughed, finally wiping the tears from his own eyes. That sounded like Elise. It had warmed his heart to see her caring for the orphan boy Ajax, who was now officially the King's heir.

The mother of a Seraph and a Prince.

"What of the Paladins?" Ren asked Arkos.

The last Lighthammer sighed and rubbed the back of his neck. Trent saw Devin in him in that moment, fleeting though it was. He hoped that Arkos would find his way out of his cousin's shadow eventually.

"Without our magic, we aren't very useful compared to the Demigods. Still, those of us left are planning on serving the kingdom somehow."

"Good," Ren said.

"We should go," Trent whispered as the door to the wagon closed.

The group clasped hands and hugged one another a final time before the Seraphs mounted their horses and made their way out of the open gate.

Outside the walls of the city, piles of corpses rotted in the midday sun. Edmund didn't want to leave the landscape littered as such, but his priorities had rightly been to focus on repairing Illux itself, first. In the coming weeks, some of those who had fled the villages would likely return to their homes, and for the most part, life on the Mortal Plane would return to normal. The people of Seatown had already returned to the east, taking the body of Gil with them. Wyn had told Trent that they planned to explore the Unnamed Sea and find new lands to populate. She also promised Edmund that there would be peace between their two countries. Trent hoped she was right.

In the distance, the Rim of Paradise loomed over them. As Trent looked at the woman who rode in silence beside him, he felt that the mountains had once again earned their name.

EPILOGUE

1055 AP

Months had passed since the siege of Illux. The fields outside the city had finally been cleared of debris, and the walls had begun to be repaired. The villages no longer sat empty as refugees returned to their homes. It was then that She felt it was time.

The woman wore a loose-fitting shawl over brown robes that wouldn't have looked out of place on a priest. She walked through the gates of Illux without pausing to marvel at its white walls. After all, had She not seen far greater things than that?

The streets of what had once been the slums still teemed with people as She walked past. None paid Her any heed. What was one more person without a home? The old hovels and shacks were being torn down and replaced with stone structures of the same sort as the inner city. She knew that the King would keep his word and erase the divide between those near the wall and those near the city's heart. She also knew that his descendants were unlikely to keep that promise.

Several youths walked by with white streaks in their hair. They were young for soldiers, but many had been enlisted by Ren when they marched for the Great Chasm. These Demigods did take notice of the woman, but shook off whatever feeling She had given them and continued on their way.

When she finally reached the plaza of the Grand Cathedral, She stopped to look around. The Grand Cathedral itself was being torn down. She knew that it was to be replaced with a palace for the King and a great meeting hall for the city assembly. Edmund had ordered that smaller churches be built throughout the city in honor of the High God, but building new homes had rightfully taken precedence.

"Bit odd, isn't it?" a man asked her.

"Why do you say that?" She replied.

She turned and saw a large dark-skinned man in white armor. He had a large hammer strapped to his back. Arkos Lighthammer. The man She had come to find.

"Our whole lives the Grand Cathedral stood here as a symbol of our devotion to the gods, and now they are dead and it's following them."

"The High God lives," She said.

He snorted.

"No offense, but the High God hasn't given two shits about us in a thousand years."

She smiled at him and walked up to what looked to be a nearby statue. It was a warrior made of metal, though the elements had dulled its sheen, and moss now covered parts of it. Tempest Born Luna had called them. She always had been the dramatic one.

"What if I showed you a miracle, Arkos Lighthammer? Would you believe then?" She asked.

The Paladin was taken aback.

"How do you know my name?" he asked.

"I know many things. I know that you search for meaning now, a way to keep your oaths and protect your people, a way to atone for your sins. I can show you how to do this."

"Who in the High God's name are you?"

She smiled.

Her hands traced the face of the Tempest Born in front of her. Luna's creation had been crude. The lesser gods could not create life whole cloth. They could change creation, but they couldn't truly make something new. These warriors had been nothing more than automatons filled with energy from her own Divine Blood. They lacked the true Divine Spark of the mortals.

"Go to the northeast, and look for the Lance of Retribution. There you will find the last gift of Kane Darksend, and what you seek."

"What are you talking about?" Arkos demanded as he stepped closer.

"A way for Paladins to connect with the Light once more. Now I ask again, would a miracle cause you to believe that the High God still watches over the Mortal Plane?" Her voice had grown firmer and dripped with power.

The Paladin found himself at a loss for words, so he merely nodded.

"Good," She said.

Then the plaza was filled with blinding light. People cried out from all sides. When the light faded, the moss had fallen from the Tempest Born, and the eyes of the metallic warrior glowed a golden white.

Arkos pulled forth his hammer and cried out. Across the plaza, more weapons were drawn as the other Tempest Born began to stir. She stepped back and placed her hand on the Paladin's arm.

"Be not afraid," She said. "I have simply given them what I once gave to you. Life, and the ability to live it as they see fit."

Then She turned and began walking back toward the walls.

Arkos called after Her, but She ignored him. She didn't like to interfere with Her creation, lest She feel like she was robbing them of the ultimate power to forge their own destinies. But sometimes, like a parent guiding a confused child, they needed a nudge in the right direction.

WHAT TO READ NEXT

To learn more about the hero Broderick Breaksword, keep an eye out for the upcoming novel *Breaksword*, from Dark Tidings Press.

For more adventures of our principle cast prior to the events of this trilogy, read the short fiction collection *Before the Breaking*.

ABOUT THE AUTHOR

Kris Jerome was born in the middle of a snowstorm in Pendleton, Oregon, several decades ago. Since then he moved the great distance across the state to study at Willamette University. He obtained a BFA in Digital Communication Arts in June of 2016 from Oregon State University. Kris enjoys reading books and comics while sipping wine and craft beer. He currently lives in Albany, Oregon with his wife, seven children and two cats.

darktidingspress.com
darktidingspress@gmail.com